DIXIE MARTIN

BY
GRACE MAY NORTH

BOSTON
LOTHROP, LEE & SHEPARD CO.

Copyright, 1902,
By Lothrop, Lee & Shepard Co.

PRINTED IN U. S. A.
Norward Press
BERWICK & SMITH CO.
NORWOOD, MASS.

Dedicated to
IVERS ASHLEY

CONTENTS

CHAPTER PAGE
I. Dixie 11
II. New Teacher 21
III. Neighborhood Gossip 27
IV. Getting Acquainted 38
V. The Woodford Schoolhouse 46
VI. Ken's Secret Sorrow 56
VII. The Blessing Undisguised 66
VIII. A Queer Bank 72
IX. The "Charity Barrel" 76
X. Carol's Choice 86
XI. Planning a Way Out 91
XII. Carol's New Home 96
XIII. Carol in Disgrace 103
XIV. The Little Runaway 109
XV. A Happy Reunion 119
XVI. A Joyous Dixie 124
XVII. A Defiant Teacher 133
XVIII. The Sheep-King Dictates 140
XIX. Dixie Goes Shopping 146
XX. Dixie Buys a Silk Dress 157
XXI. Dixie Visits a Friend 162
XXII. Teacher Revolutionizes 166
XXIII. The Return of Topsy 175
XXIV. Dixie's Lesson in Dressmaking 180
XXV. Where the Trail Led 191
XXVI. Ken's Qust 196
XXVII. Celebrating 205
XXVIII. On the Trail of a "Bandit" 209
XXIX. Ken's Old Friend 222
XXX. "Rattlesnake Sam" 232
XXXI. An Unwelcome Guest 238
XXXII. A Hard Game 248
XXXIII. Rude Little Sylvia 256
XXXIV. The Young Engineer Dreams 263
XXXV. The Pretend Game 269
XXXVI. Ken's Talk With Teacher 283
XXXVII. Carol's Birthday S'prise 288
XXXVIII. The Expected Blizzard 302
XXXIX. A Happy Father 312
XL. A Mystery Solved 319
XLI. A Resolution Broken 328
XLII. An Eventful Spring 337
XLIII. The Unexpected Guest 347
XLIV. Clearing Up Mysteries 353

DIXIE MARTIN
CHAPTER ONE
DIXIE

"Carolina Martin, you get up this instant. Do you hear me? I've called you sixteen times already, if 'tisn't twenty, and *this* the morning the new teacher starts at the old log schoolhouse over at Woodford's. You don't want us all to be late, do you, and have her think we're shiftless, like the poor white folks our mother used to tell about, in the mountains down in Tennessee. We, with the bluest blood in our veins that flows in the whole South! Carolina, *are you up?*"

This conversation was carried on in a high-pitched voice by a thin, homely, freckled-faced little girl whose straight brick-red hair had not a wave in it, and whose long, skinny legs, showing beneath the gingham dress two years too short for her, made her appear as ungainly as a colt.

There was no one else present in the big living-room of the log cabin, but the voice carried well, and was heard in the loft above, where, in a large four-posted bed, another small girl sleepily replied, "Oh, Dixie, I wish folks never did have to get up, nor go to school, nor—" The voice trailed off drowsily, and Carolina had just turned over for another little nap when she heard her sister climbing the ladder which led from the room below to the loft where the two girls slept.

Instantly the culprit leaped to the floor. When the red head of Dixie appeared at the square opening of the trap-door, the small girl was making great haste to don her one piece of all-over underwear.

She smiled her sweetest at her irate sister, whose wrath softened, for little Carolina was so like their beautiful mother. Even at eight years of age she had the languid manner of the South, and spoke with a musical drawl.

But there was no envy in the heart of the older girl. She was passionately glad that one of them was so like that adored mother who had died soon after the birth of her youngest child, who now was four years old.

The father, an honest, hardy Nevada mountaineer, had been killed in a raid two years later, and since then Dixie, aged twelve, had been little mother and home-maker for the other three children.

Before Dixie could rebuke the younger sister, a door below opened and a baby voice called shrilly, "Oh, Dix, do come quick! Suthin's a-runnin' over on the stove."

"It's the porridge." The older girl sniffed the air, which conveyed to her the scent of something burning. Down the ladder she scrambled.

"Well, lucky stars!" she exclaimed a moment later as she removed the kettle and gave the contents a vigorous stirring.

"'Tisn't stuck to the bottom, that's one comfort." Then, whirling about, she caught the little four-year-old boy in her arms as she exclaimed, "And so our Jimmikins is going to school to-day for the very first time."

The small head, covered with sunny curls, nodded, and his eyes twinkled as he proudly prattled: "I'll stan' up front and I'll spell c-a-t, and ever'thin', won't I, Dixie?"

"Of course you will, pet lamb, and maybe the teacher will ask you to recite, and won't she be surprised to find that you know seven speaking pieces?"

While Dixie talked she was dishing up the porridge. She glanced at the ladder and sighed. Would she have to climb it again? What *could* be keeping Carolina? But just then a foot appeared and slowly there descended the member of the family who was always late. She had been brushing her soft golden-brown curls in front of their one mirror. A pretty circling comb held them in place.

Carol wore a faded gingham dress which was buttoned in the front, that she might fasten it herself.

There was a discontented expression in her violet eyes.

"I just hate this ol' dress," she began fretfully. "Jessica Archer doesn't believe we have any blue blood at all, or we'd want to dress like the Southern ladies do in the pictures."

Dixie sighed, and the younger girl, who thought only of herself, continued, "If my beautiful mother had lived, she wouldn't have let me wear shabby dresses that button down the front and make everybody laugh at me."

There was much truth in this. Their beautiful mother would have been quite willing to mortgage the ranch if only she and her children could be dressed in silk and furbelows.

Before Dixie could reply, the cabin-door again opened, and in came a boy who was at least a head taller than Dixie. His frank, freckled face was smiling. He was carrying a pail. "Dix," he said gleefully, "we're going to have a real crop of apples this year. I've been down to the creek-bottom to see how the trees are doing. Maybe they'll fetch in money enough so that you can buy that new stove you've been needing so long."

Carolina tossed her curly head as she thought, "Stove, indeed, when I need a new dress." But she said nothing. The apples weren't ripe yet, and she could bide her time.

They were soon seated around the table, chattering eagerly about the new teacher who had arrived at Woodford's the day before, but whom, as yet, they had not seen.

"What you 'spose she'll be like?" Ken asked as he helped himself to the rich creamy goat's milk, and then turned to pour more of it into the big bowl for his little brother, who had been hungrily clamoring for porridge.

Carol sniffed. "I don't like new teachers," she informed them in a manner much older than her years. "They're always startin' somethin' different."

"You mean that new teachers don't like *you*," Ken put in with brotherly frankness. "They would, though, if you'd ever study, which I reckon you *never* will."

"You'd ought to learn all you can, Caroly. We all ought to," the little mother modified, "'cause as soon as we're old enough, we'll want to be earning our own living so we won't always be poor and scrimping like we are now."

Carolina tossed her curls.

"'Twon't be needful for *me* to earn my livin'," she said proudly. "Mrs. Piggins says I'm the kind that always marries young, and I'm goin' to marry rich, too."

Ken exploded with amused laughter.

"Hear the baby prattle!" he teased. "You'd better be thinkin' about your dolls, seems like to me."

The all-too-easily-aroused temper of the younger girl flared.

"Ken Martin, you know I haven't played with dolls, not since I was seven years old, and now I'm eight."

The violet eyes flashed and the pretty lips quivered.

The heart of Ken always melted when he saw tears.

"Oh, I say, Caroly," he begged. "Don't get a mad on. Honest Injun, cross my heart, I won't tease you any more——er——that is, not again this morning, anyhow," he added, wishing to be truthful.

Then, knowing from past experience that the best way to dry up tears was to interest the doleful one in something different, he exclaimed as though he had suddenly thought of it: "Girls, what'll we give as a present for new teacher? The fellows were all sayin' yesterday what they're goin' to give."

The ruse worked like a charm. Carol looked across the table at her brother with eager interest.

"That horrid Jessica Archer says there's nobody in the school as is going to give new teacher as handsome a present as she is. Her mother took her over to Reno to pick it out. Jessica says as all the other pupils will give country presents, but hers'll be *city*."

"Huh!" grunted the older brother. "What's that little minx goin' to give teacher that's so fine? That's what I'd like to know."

The curls were shaken as the owner of them replied: "She won't tell. It's a secret, but she's boastin' as it cost more'n all the other presents put together'll cost."

"Well, dearie, like as not she's right," the older girl said soothingly. "Jessica Archer's father's the richest man anywhere in these mountains. You know how folks call him a sheep-king."

Then, as Dixie was always trying to have her charges see things in the right way, she continued: "Anyhow, it isn't the money a present costs that counts. It's the love that goes with it."

Selfish Carol was not convinced. "I'd rather have a blue silk dress *without* love than I would another ol' gingham like this one with—"

She was interrupted by Ken, who burst in with: "Oh, I say, Dix, I've just thought of the peachiest present. You know that little black-and-white kid that came a while ago."

The girls had stopped eating, and were listening with eyes as well as ears.

"Yeah, I know, b-but what of it?" Dixie inquired.

The boy's words fairly tumbled out in his excitement.

"I bet teacher'd like *him* for a present. I bet she would. Like as not, comin' from New York City the way she does, she's never had a goat for a pet, and this one's awful pretty, with that white star on his black forehead."

Dixie looked uncertain. "It *would* be different, but—" she started to protest, when noting her brother's crestfallen expression, she hastened to add, "Come to think of it, now, a little goat might be lots of company for new teacher, she being so strange and all.

"You go get the goat, Ken, and saddle Pegasus while I tidy up the kitchen and dress Jimmikins. Then we'll all be ready to start for school."

"I've got an ol' red ribbon that'll look handsome on that little goat's neck," Carol told them. "That'll make it look more presentish, seems like."

"Of course it will, dear. Go get it and give it to Ken, though I guess maybe you'd better tie the bow. You've got a real knack at making them pretty."

The little mother always tried to show appreciation of any talent that might appear, however faintly, in one of her precious brood.

A moment later all was hurry and scurry in the homey kitchen of that old log house, for this was a red-letter morning in the lives of the four little Martins.

CHAPTER TWO
NEW TEACHER

And the new teacher, what of her? She had arrived by stage the night before, after a long journey across the country to Reno by train, and from there over rough roads of the wonderful Sierra Nevada mountains, and, just at nightfall, she had been deposited, bag and baggage, in front of a rambling old road-house known as Woodford's Inn. It had been too dark for her really to see anything but the deep abyss of blackness below, that was the cañon through which she had just ridden, and the peaks of the rugged range towering above her, the dazzling stars that seemed so much nearer than they had in the East, and the lights of the comfortable and welcoming inn toward which the stage-driver was leading her.

Mrs. Enterprise Twiggly, the innkeeper's wife, a thin, angular woman, whose reddish-gray hair was drawn tightly back, and whose dress was economical in the extreme, as it boasted neither pleat nor fullness, appeared in the open door, and her greenish-blue eyes appraised the guest at a glance. Long training had taught Mrs. Enterprise Twiggly to know at once whether to offer a new arrival the best bedroom or the slant-walled one over the kitchen.

The sharp, business-like expression changed to one of real pleasure when the innkeeper's wife beheld the newcomer. She advanced, with a bony work-hardened hand outstretched. "Well! I declare to it, if I'm not mistaken, and I never am, this here is the new teacher. I am Mrs. Enterprise Twiggly of the Woodford's Inn. Like as not you've heard of me. I'm that glad you've come, Miss Bayley. Do you want to go right to your shack, or would you rather stay at the inn, where there's folks, until you get used to the strange night noises?"

Miss Josephine Bayley, late of the city of New York, marveled at the remark, for never before had she been conscious of such intense stillness.

"I have indeed heard of you, Mrs. Twiggly," the girl declared, and truly, for the letter she had received from the board had mentioned that she would live near the inn. "I'm sure that I am going to just adore your wonderful mountain country." Then, realizing that she had not replied to the query of her hostess, she added, "I am perfectly willing to sleep in my own apartment, that is—shack, did you call it?"

The tall angular woman nodded. "Enterprise!" she then called to a short, apologetic-looking man who was serving sandwiches and coffee to the stage-driver in the dining-room of the inn. "Fetch the key that's hangin' by the stove, and maybe you'd better fetch along some matches and a candle, too."

"Ye-ah, I'll be there directly." Which he was. Taking a large suit-case in one hand, and a lighted lantern in the other, he led the way, and his wife followed with another suit-case. The stage-driver, at the end of the procession, had a steamer-trunk over his shoulder. Mr. Twiggly opened the door and stepped back to permit his wife to enter first. This she was about to do, when, remembering her manners, she, too, stepped back to permit the school-teacher to go first, and so it was that Josephine Bayley entered the log cabin that was to be her home for she knew not how long.

How she wanted to sink down on the nearest rocker and laugh, for the mirth within seemed determined to bubble over, but when she glanced at the angular, business-like Mrs. Enterprise Twiggly, the new school-teacher knew that laughter would be greatly misunderstood, and so she managed to remark meekly, "I am sure that this will be a very pleasant apartment,—that is, I mean, shack."

She looked about the large square room, wondering where she was to sleep. Mrs. Twiggly surmised as much, and, as soon as the men were gone, she said rather disparagingly: "The last teacher we had was the new-fangled kind from down Los Angeles way, and nothing would do but she had to have what she called a screen-porch bedroom built, and bein' as she paid for it herself, the board couldn't keep her from doin' it. Too, she was set on havin' it on the offside from the inn, which seemed queer to me. You'd have thought she'd built it next to where folks was, but she said she liked to feel that she was 'way off by herself in the mountains. Howsomever, she always kept a loaded six-shooter handy in the corner."

As she talked, the woman led the way through a door, and the girl, advancing, uttered an exclamation of delight, for she found herself on a porch so open that she was hardly conscious that there were walls. "Oh," she thought, "blessings on the head of my predecessor, outlandish though she may have seemed to mine hostess!"

Mrs. Twiggly was eyeing her curiously. "You like it?" she inquired, rather hoping that she would not. She decided that all teaching folk were hopeless, when Josephine Bayley turned around with eyes that glowed, and, clasping her hands, exclaimed, "I never had such a perfectly wonderful place to sleep in all my whole life!"

Mrs. Twiggly's sniff was not audible. "What poor folks she must come from!" she was thinking. Aloud she remarked: "Miss Bayley, I'll fetch over your breakfast to-morrow, bein' as it's your first mornin', and if you're scared, fire off the gun twice, but mind you aim it in the air. Well, good-night."

"Good-night, and thank you for your kindness." Then Josephine Bayley was left alone with the stars and the silence, but somehow her desire to laugh was gone. She felt awed by the bigness and stillness of things, and standing in the darkness in her out-of-doors bedroom, she reached her arms toward the star-crowned peaks and prayed, "God of the mountains, give me *here* some work to do for You."

CHAPTER THREE
NEIGHBORHOOD GOSSIP

Josephine Bayley awakened, as all do in entirely new surroundings, with the question, "Why, where am I?" Then, upon hearing a chattering of animal life without, she sat up in bed and saw a fir tree festooned with webs that sparkled with quivering dewdrops, saw two bushy-tailed squirrels gathering cones, and heard a meadow-lark singing its joyous morning-song. The new teacher arose, surprised to find that all that night she had not awakened. She glanced in the corner where stood the sentinel gun. She was sure that she should never have need of its services.

Just as she was dressed she heard a rapping on her outer door. Skipping, with a heart as light as her feet, she opened it, and beheld Mrs. Enterprise Twiggly standing there with a tray. She looked exactly as she had the night before, only more so, in the full light of all-revealing day.

[28]

"Good-mornin', Miss Bayley," the woman remarked, as she entered the sun-flooded living-room of the log cabin and placed the tray on the rustic center-table.

"I didn't hear any firin' in the night, so I take it you slept through."

"I did, indeed," was the enthusiastic reply. "No longer shall I need a pine pillow to woo slumber. I don't know when I have awakened so refreshed."

Then the girl added with a happy laugh: "The truth is, I didn't know what I was supposed to be afraid of, and so, of course, I couldn't be afraid of it."

This remark sounded a little unbalanced to the wife of the innkeeper. She had never heard that one had to know what to be afraid of before he could be afraid. She drew herself up very straight as she enumerated: "Well, there's plenty that usually scares tenderfoot school-teachers. There's the coyotes howlin' at night, though they mostly never touches human bein's; an' now and then there's a bear, but worst, I guess, is the parcel of Indians over Tahoe way. They don't do much but thievin'. I guess that's all, unless 'tis now and then a bandit passin' this way to hold up a train over beyond Reno."

[29]

Scandalized, indeed, was the wife of the innkeeper when she heard the new school-teacher laugh. "Oh, Mrs. Twiggly," the girl exclaimed merrily, "I do hope some one of those skeery things will happen soon. I'm just longing for adventure."

This time the sniff of her listener was entirely audible. "Well, I reckon you'll get all the adventure you're wantin' before the term's up, Miss Bayley, if you're kept, and I sort o' feel it my duty to tell you that the board of eddication hereabouts is particular and persnifity."

"Which means?" was what Miss Bayley thought. But aloud she demurely asked, "Mrs. Twiggly, just what are the requirements that I shall have to meet?"

[30]

The wife of the innkeeper bristled, as she always did when this subject was discussed. "If you mean what you ought to do to please the board, I must say it seems like there's nothin' needed but just to flatter and pamper the board's only child, that forward little Jessica Archer."

Miss Bayley's dark eyes were wide. "Is there only *one* man on the local board of education?" she inquired.

Mrs. Twiggly nodded. "Ye-ah, and, for that matter, there's only *one* important man in these here parts, and that's Mr. Sethibald Archer. He owns all the sheep-grazin' country round about, and if he don't own it *honest*, he's got it somehow."

"Sethibald?" Miss Bayley repeated. "I never heard such a Christian name as that before."

Mrs. Twiggly was scornful.

"Well, 'twa'n't that in the beginnin'," she said. "It was jest plain Seth, but when they got so rich, his wife, who'd allus been Maria, went to visit folks in the city, and when she came back she had her name printed on bits of pasteboard, visitin'-cards, she called 'em, though land knows who she's goin' to visit in these parts, and she said Mrs. Seth didn't look stylish enough, so she tacked on the endin'. Mrs. Sethibald Archer, that's what's on the card."

[31]

Again the new teacher had an almost uncontrollable desire to laugh, but, instead, she seated herself at the table and ate the really good breakfast, and found that she was unusually hungry. The mountain-air surely was a tonic.

As her guest seemed in no hurry to depart, Miss Bayley said, "Won't you be seated, Mrs. Twiggly, and tell me some more about my duties as school-teacher?"

"Well, I dunno but I can set a spell," was the reply of the garrulous woman, who had "talked herself thin," as Mrs. Sethibald Archer had been known to declare, and which may have been true.

"Please tell me about my other pupils," Miss Bayley continued.

There was a visible stiffening of the form of Mrs. Twiggly. "I'll tell you first about the four children who live down in Woodford's Cañon, them as had a shiftless, do-nothin'-useful actress for a mother."

[32]

And so it was that Miss Josephine Bayley first heard of brave little Dixie Martin and her three young charges.

"'Twas the year of the big blizzard," Mrs. Twiggly began, sitting so stiff and straight that her listener found herself wondering if she had a poker for a backbone. "I declare to it, there never had been such a winter. Too, that was the year they struck silver over beyond the cañon. It got out that the mountains hereabouts were all chock-full of payin' ore, and overnight, it seemed like, a minin'-camp sprung up and grew in a fortnight to be a reg'lar town with houses and stores and even a the-*a*-ter built. You can see the ruins of it now when you're over that way, and, havin' a the-*a*-ter brought play-actin' folks to Silver City, and mighty big money they took in.

"It came easy, and was spent easy, but all of a sudden there was no more silver; the veins had petered out, and the gay life of that town blew out like the flame on a candle, and then it was that some little one-horse show, havin' heard how rich other actors had struck it there, came trailin' along, but they was too late.

[33]

"They gave their show,—'Shakespeare,' they called it,—but they gave it to empty benches. They'd come over from Reno on the stage all dressed up in their hifalutin' costumes, so's not to have to fetch over their trunks, but they didn't have any money to pay their way back, and so they started to walk.

"Well, one of 'em was a pretty, frail-lookin' young girl, with big round eyes and soft curly hair. She wore a long, trailin' white dress. Ophelia, they called her, but she wa'n't strong, and them paper shoes she had on got cut to pieces as soon as she began to walk along the mountain roads. When they got to Woodford's Cañon the man dressed up as king saw as she couldn't walk any farther, so he said she'd have to stop at some ranch-house and rest till the stage-coach came along.

[34]

"The only house anywhere near belonged to Pine Tree Martin. Folks hereabouts called him that because he was always sayin', 'Neighbors, don't cut down the pine trees.' Queer, how that man did love pine trees. He had two of the finest ones you ever saw growin' in front of his log cabin, and they're still there. Well, Pine Tree Martin was nigh forty years old, and he'd been livin' alone since his ol' mother died. The king and another fellow they called Hamlet went to the cabin and knocked on the door. Nobody was at home, so they pushed open the door and found a fire burning in the stove and supper set for one on the table. They carried Ophelia, who had fainted by that time, into the cabin and put her on the bed, then the rest of them made tracks for Reno."

The sniff was very audible now.

Then she went on: "That shows how much morals play-actin' folks have, but I can tell you Pine Tree Martin wa'n't made of no such ne'er-do-well stuff. When he found that done-up girl with her big round eyes and soft curly hair in his house, and heerd how she didn't have a home that she could go to, he up and loved her, as only the Pine Tree Martin kind of people can love.

[35]

"He married her and took the tenderest sort o' care of her as long as she lived. Nothin' he could get was too good for her, and she as useless as a—well, a butterfly, I guess. An' what's more, she was allus talkin' about what blue-blooded folks her relations was. It seems their name was Haddington-Allen, and they was rich and proud. They had disowned her because she wanted to go on the stage and be a star. When Dixie was born, she wrote letters to the aunt that had fetched her up in the South, but they allus came back, and on 'em was written, 'Unopened by Mrs. Haddington-Allen.'

"This Mrs. Pine Tree Martin never took to Western ways. Her heart was allus in the South, an' as her children were born she named them Dixie, Carolina, and Kentucky, till the baby came, and she named him after the uncle that had fetched her up, James Haddington-Allen Martin.

[36]

"In one way it turned out good for Dixie to have such a shiftless mother, for as soon as that girl could hold a saucepan she began to cook for the family. The only thing the mother would do was sew, and she made fancy dresses for herself and for the other girl, Carolina, to wear. She never took much pride in the two older children. The boy, Ken, was the livin' image of his homely, raw-boned pa, and Dixie was a great disappointment, for she was a Martin clear through, but Carolina was the picture of her ma, and still is, and just like her.

"Well, when James Haddington-Allen Martin was three months old, the mother died, and the father was left with four children, which was bad enough, but two years later Pine Tree Martin was killed in a raid, and since then Dixie, who's just come twelve, has kept house and been mother to the other three," Mrs. Twiggly concluded.

Then, before Josephine Bayley could comment on the sad story that she had just heard, Mrs. Twiggly arose. "I declare to it," she exclaimed, "if 'tisn't eight o'clock and you'll want to be startin' to school early. Follow the road right down toward the cañon, then turn toward the mountains a bit, and there you are. You'd better not step off the road to-day. There's adders and rattlers hereabouts. You'll get so you can tell a coiled snake from a stone arter you've been here a spell, but just at first you'd better be keerful."

[37]

Then when she reached the door with the tray she turned to say condescendingly: "I'm real glad you've come, Miss Bayley. It's mighty nice to have folks as interesting as you are to talk to, an' I do hope the board will like you."

She was out of the door when she stepped back to add: "Miss Bayley, if it don't come too hard, I'd sort of let it seem like you think Jessica Archer is prettier than Carolina Martin and smarter than Dixie. It'll be stretchin' the truth mighty hard, but it's policy. Good mornin', Miss Bayley."

The new teacher, at last alone, put her hands to her head as though she felt dizzy. How rasping was Mrs. Twiggly's voice! But a moment later she was thinking of the poor little children of that stranded Ophelia, and looked eagerly forward to her first meeting with them.

[38]

CHAPTER FOUR
GETTING ACQUAINTED

It was a perfect autumn day, and he who has not been in the Sierra Nevada mountains on a golden October morning has not as yet known the full joy of living.

Josephine Bayley had been advised to lock her door in order to keep out "snoopin' Indians." She had been shown through a field-glass a group of most dilapidated dwellings about a mile to the south and down in the creek-bottom. These dwellings could not be called wigwams; indeed, they were too nondescript really to be called anything. Some had a rough framework of saplings, with pine branches for a roof and walls; others were made of stones held together with mud, while still others were but shiftlessly erected tents, even discarded clothing having been used, and all were surrounded by rubbish and squalor. Thus the one-time picturesqueness of the Washoe Indian has degenerated.

"They're curious and snoopin', those Indians are, but harmless," Mrs. Enterprise Twiggly had said, when advising Miss Bayley to keep her door locked while she was away.

The new teacher, lithe, dark, athletic, stepped springily down the mountain road, feeling as though she must sing with a lark that was somewhere over in a clump of murmuring pines. But the first note of the song died on her lips as she suddenly stopped and gazed ahead of her.

Had that stone in the road moved, or was it her imagination? She gazed fascinated. Was it about to uncoil and raise a protesting head? Gracious! What was it she had heard about rattlers? When they coiled, they could spring—how far—was it twice the length of their own bodies? Did one have to measure them to know how far away one could stand in safety? If they were straight out, one always had time to escape, for they had to coil to strike. But the large round stone that did look strangely like a coiled snake did not stir, not even when a smaller rock was thrown at it.

Miss Bayley, laughing at her own fears, looked down the cañon road ahead of her, where she beheld a little procession approaching. A light of recognition brightened her dark eyes. "Oh, I am so glad!" she thought. "Here come the children of Ophelia."

A queer-looking group they made. There was a soft mouse-colored burro, and on it sat a truly beautiful little girl of eight years, holding in front of her a chubby four-year-old boy, who was beaming with delight. A tall, lank lad, with a staff in one hand, was guiding the beast of burden, while on the other side, with pride shining in her eyes, that were a warm golden-brown, walked the little mother of them all, Dixie Martin. She was carrying a basket that held their lunch and leading a very small, long-legged goat that had a red ribbon tied about its neck.

As they emerged from the dark cañon road into the full sunlight beyond the great old pines they beheld for the first time their new teacher. They knew at once that it must be she, and Ken snatched off his cap, while little Carolina, slipping from the back of the burro, made a graceful curtsy, just as her mother had trained her to do from babyhood. Dixie, too, had been trained, but she was a Martin, and did not take to polishing as readily as did Carol.

The new teacher hurried forward with hands outstretched. She actually forgot to examine the stones in the road that might be coiled snakes.

"Oh, you dear little pupils of mine!" she exclaimed. "You are the four Martins, aren't you?"

"Yes, ma'am, we are," was the chorused reply; and then it was that Miss Bayley recalled that even the best people in the South say "ma'am."

[42]

Carolina, wishing to shine, stepped forward and said: "I'll introduce us, shall I? This is my big sister, Dixie Martin, and our baby brother, Jimmy-Boy." Then the small girl held herself proudly, as the mother had done, as she added, "His real name is James Haddington-Allen Martin, after our aunt who is blue-blooded in the South."

There was a sudden flush in the freckled face of the older girl, and she hastened to say apologetically: "Miss Bayley, please pardon my little sister for saying that. I've told her time and again that when folks are truly blue-blooded it shows without their telling it." Then she added, as she nodded toward the boy who stood waiting his turn, "This is our big brother, Ken, and I guess that's all the introducing, unless Pegasus ought to be mentioned."

"Pegasus?" the new teacher repeated as she gazed at the stolid little burro and marveled. "Pray, what do you kiddies know about Pegasus?" Even as she spoke she realized that much that was unusual might be expected from the children of Ophelia.

It was Dixie who said eagerly, "Oh, our beautiful mother wrote the loveliest poetry, and she used to say that the wonderful winged horse, Pegasus, carried her to the Land of Inspiration."

[43]

Miss Bayley noticed that the small goat had not been introduced. Ken, believing that the moment for the presentation was at hand, took the leading-rope from his sister, and, stepping forward, he said, almost shyly: "Miss Bayley, teacher, we fetched along Star-White as your present. We thought maybe you'd like him for a pet."

It had been said of Miss Josephine Bayley that she could rise to any occasion without evidencing surprise or dismay, and she surely did at this moment. Luckily, her practice-work on the East Side in New York had taught her to expect the most extraordinary gifts from her pupils.

The four pairs of eyes watched anxiously for a moment. *Would "new teacher" like their present?*

[44]

Their doubts were quickly put to flight, for Miss Josephine Bayley stooped and caressed the long-legged, rather startled kid as she said with a ring of real enthusiasm in her voice: "You dear Star-White, you're as nice as you can be. I just know that I'm going to love you." Then, rising, she held out a hand to the two who were nearest, but the others were included in her smiling glance as she said: "Thank you so much, dears. It was ever so kind of you to want to make me happy." Then, a little helplessly, she appealed to the older boy as she asked, "What shall we do with Star-White now?"

"I'll tie him up in the shed back o' your cabin, Miss Bayley. He'll be all right in there."

The lad skipped ahead, the kid in his arms, but returned in an incredibly short time.

The procession had continued on its way, and Ken soon remarked, "There's the schoolhouse, teacher, down the piney lane, and I think there's folks waiting to see you."

Miss Bayley turned and saw, back from the road and on a short lane, a log schoolhouse half hidden by great old pines. In front of it stood a very fine carriage drawn by two milk-white horses. At their heads a stocky man with a stubby red beard and a keen, alert, red-brown eye awaited her. He was the "board of education," of that Miss Bayley was sure, while on the back seat of the vehicle, with her bonneted head held high, sat no less a personage than Mrs. Sethibald Archer, and at her side, also with her head held high, was a much-beruffled young girl, aged eight years, who was of course the prettiest and smartest child in the school. Miss Bayley assured herself that she mustn't forget that, not for one moment, if she wanted to stay, and, oh, how she did want to stay and get acquainted with the wonderful mountains, and the Martins, and maybe even with the Indians who lived down in the creek-bottom!

All this she thought as she walked up the little lane toward the old log schoolhouse.

CHAPTER FIVE
THE WOODFORD SCHOOLHOUSE

Mr. Sethibald Martin advanced with what he believed to be a dignified stride. Without removing his hat, he said, "This here is Miss Josephine Bayley, I take it—her as has credentials to teach correct speakin' and figurin'."

A voice from the vehicle was heard. "You'd better look at 'em, Sethibald, to make sure. I don't want no teacher that can't learn my Jessica correct speakin', such as will fit her for the high sphere she is to fill as the daughter of a sheep-king." The speech had been planned, that the new teacher might at once be impressed with the importance of the Archers in that mountain community.

The stubby gentleman seemed actually to puff up a bit, "as a toad might," the newcomer found herself thinking, but, remembering his present mission, he explained the duties and requirements of the position, then added, as he glanced almost scornfully at the silent, listening group of four children and a burro, "It sure is onfortunate. Miss Bayley, that the pupils from these here parts are so no-account, my own Jessica bein' exceptionated."

His glance turned with pride to the snub-nosed child in the buggy. Then, in a whispered aside: "It's lucky for you that you've got one promisin' pupil like my daughter, Miss Bayley. 'Twould be dull work teachin' if you didn't have nothin' but dumb young 'uns like those Pine Tree Martins." He paused, seeming to expect comment. This, then, was Miss Bayley's moment for being diplomatic.

"I am sure that I shall find your little daughter a very receptive pupil, Mr. Archer," she said graciously. This time it was certain that Mr. Sethibald had puffed. He had never heard the word "receptive" before, but it had a most complimentary sound.

[48]

"Yes, ma'am, Miss Bayley, you'll find the little sheep-princess all that an' more, much more, ma'am." He was unctuously rubbing his hands as he spoke. Then going to the side of the vehicle and holding out a bediamonded hand, he added, "Come now, Jessica, darlin', and meet the new teacher, her as is goin' to teach you lots of nice things."

He lifted the small girl to the ground, and Miss Bayley advanced, her hand held out, but the little "sheep-princess" drew back and clung to her father.

The teacher found herself comparing this lack of manners with the natural graciousness of Carolina, but the father evidently considered his daughter's behavior as being praiseworthy.

"Shy little thing," he commented in another of his quite audible asides. "Not bold like that Carry Martin."

Then the unexpected happened. The little girl referred to darted forward with catlike swiftness. "My name is *not* Carry Martin," she cried. "It's Carolina, and my folks are—" She was drawn back and quieted by poor Dixie, who looked her misery. Teacher, quite at a loss what to say, glanced at the shy and model Jessica at that moment and saw her sticking out her tongue and tilting her nose at the Martins.

[49]

Miss Bayley sighed. There were evidently snags ahead, but Mrs. Archer was speaking. "Sethibald," she said, with a desire to impress the new teacher with her own great importance, "it's time now that you were a-drivin' me over to Genoa, where I have to speak in front of a mothers' meetin' on how to bring up the young." Then, turning to Miss Bayley, she added condescendingly, "Me and you'll be great friends, I'm sure, bein' as we're both sot on upliftin' folks in this here neighborhood from shiftlessness and ignorance."

Before the astonished young teacher could reply, the stubby, reddish gentleman had climbed up on the front seat, and the restive white horses had started off down the pine-edged lane at a brisk speed, and Josephine Bayley, not knowing whether to laugh or cry, led the way into the large bare room of the old schoolhouse, where she was to spend many a day finding new problems and new pleasures. There were ten pupils in all. Two of them, Mercedes and Franciscito Guadalupe, had but recently come to that mountain country from Mexico.

[50]

Their father was the new overseer at the Archer ranch, and as yet they had not learned one word of English.

They were brightly dressed, dark-skinned little creatures, and each time that the new teacher spoke to them, their reply was the same, "*Muchas gracias, Senorita,*" which sounded very polite, but how was Josephine Bayley to teach them reading and spelling if neither knew the language of the other?

Two of the remaining pupils were equally hopeless, being the most forlorn little mites, children of a trapper who lived somewhere over toward Lake Tahoe, but, as Miss Bayley was to find, these pupils only came now and then, when their trapper-father could spare time to bring them, one in front and one back of him, on his horse.

[51]

Maggie and Millie Mullet were twins, aged six years, and Miss Bayley found as the weeks went by that although, after an hour of earnest effort, she might teach them to spell such words as "cat," "bat," "rat," "mat," when questioned the next day their minds were as blank as though they had never heard the words.

The tenth pupil was a very large boy, sixteen years of age, who was the only son of the burly blacksmith over at Woodford's. He studied diligently, and when he once learned a thing he seemed never to forget it, and so of him Miss Bayley had a little more hope. However, his father, the powerful Ira Jenkins, Senior, thought "larnin'" unnecessary, but the mother, having learned to read, pored over novels, even when preparing meals, and she had decided that her overgrown son should be a preacher like the one who came once a month from Genoa and held "meetin's" in the parlor at the inn.

As Miss Josephine Bayley looked over her little class that first morning, she felt desperately at a loss to know how to begin. Each child, it seemed, was studying something different from all the others, and, to add to her discomfort, the new teacher realized that the eyes of Jessica Archer, which were like her father's, were watching her every move as though she had been admonished by her elders to observe and report all that happened.

[52]

The one bright spot was the corner where the wide-awake, intelligent young Martins sat, and Josephine Bayley found herself actually glad that they were "blue-blooded."

Just as the new teacher was becoming almost panicky at the newness of everything, the slim, freckled hand of Dixie Martin appeared on high, and when Miss Bayley nodded, that small maiden arose, and, going to the desk on the platform, she said softly, "Please, teacher, we usually begin with singing. We all know the 'Good-Morning' song. I'll lead if you want me to; I often do."

"Oh, I'd be ever so grateful if you would."

And so Dixie turned around and began to sing, in a clear, bird-like voice, a simple little melody that the older pupils knew and sang with her. There were four stanzas, and when the song was finished, the hand of Jessica Archer went up, and, rising, she said that as she was the smartest pupil in the school, she was always asked to read first.

[53]

"Very well, Jessica. My pupils, I am sure, will all be glad to help their new teacher to-day by making suggestions. Now, if you will read where you left off last term, I shall better understand how to class you."

"Oh, I am class A," the small girl said proudly, "and Dixie Martin and Ken and Ira Jenkins are class B, and the rest are class C."

"Indeed!" was all the new teacher said, but she was thinking that her predecessor had evidently succeeded in fulfilling all the requirements of the board. But why, then, had she left? Oh, she did recall that Mrs. Enterprise Twiggly had said that the last teacher had married a prospector, who, for a time, had been in the mountains near Woodfords.

Romance was something that interested Josephine Bayley, aged twenty years, not at all. She had never been in love and never would be, she was sure of that. She was going to be wedded to her profession. She had never even met a lad who could interest her, and surely if she had failed to find one in the city of New York, where she had many delightful friends, she would not find him in this wild, rugged mountain country.

[54]

And all the while these thoughts were idly passing through the brain of Josephine Bayley, her "smartest" pupil was stumbling and stuttering through a short story in the Fourth Reader. It was not until the little girl sat down and was casting a triumphant glance over toward the Martin corner that the new teacher, with a start, awakened from her reverie.

Dixie Martin read next, and with so much expression that Miss Bayley was both amused and interested. She believed, and truly, that the mother's yearning to be an actress had descended as real talent to at least this one of her children.

"Dixie," the new teacher said, "I wish you would remain in at recess. I want to speak to you."

If there was a jealous tilt to the curly head of Jessica, Miss Bayley did not notice it. When the others had filed out, for fifteen minutes of freedom, the new teacher took the hand of Dixie and said earnestly: "Dear, why are you reading in a Third Reader? Here is a Sixth Reader. See if you couldn't read that."

[55]

The gold-brown eyes were glowing. "Oh, yes, ma'am, Miss Bayley, I could. I love reading. After supper every night I read to the children 'Pilgrim's Progress' and 'Oliver Twist' and the Almanac. That's all the books we have."

There was a firmer line about the mouth of Josephine Bayley. She had in that moment decided that she would tutor at least this one of the Martins, out of school-hours. Over her free time, surely, the board would have no jurisdiction.

CHAPTER SIX
KEN'S SECRET SORROW

It was Saturday, which was the busiest of the whole week in Woodford's Cañon, for it was house-cleaning day in the old log cabin which was guarded by two spreading pine trees, but this Saturday was especially busy.

"Carol, please do stop frittering," Dixie called as she turned from the stove which she was polishing with as much care as though it had been a piano. "Don't you know who is coming to call this very afternoon, and I'd feel just terrible, I certainly would, if Miss Bayley sat on dust, and that's what she's likely to do if you skip places at dusting, as you usually do, and I haven't time to-day to rub them over and see."

The younger girl, who had been leaning far out the window, supposedly to shake a duster, but who had continued to linger there, watching two squirrels playing tag among the dry pine needles, returned reluctantly to the task she so disliked.

"O dear! it's just mean-hateful being poor folks the way we are," she complained, "and having to do our own work with our own hands. I've heard my beautiful mother say so time and again. When she was a girl she had two little darkies to wait on her. She never had to pick up anything, if she dropped it. She didn't have to even lift a finger."

Dixie straightened up to rest her tired shoulders, for polishing a stove was hard work at best, and almost unconsciously she glanced down at her own fingers that were jet-black just then, and for a bit of a moment she sighed, and was half tempted to think that, maybe after all, it would be nice to have nothing to do but sing and read, or live in the out-of-doors that she so loved. But a second later she was her own optimistic, practical self. "Carol Martin," she announced, "just for that, now, we're going to count our blessings. You begin! One?"

"O dear!" the other little maid sighed as she knelt to dust the rungs of an old grandfather's chair. "I 'spose I ought to be thankful that I'm beautiful, like my mother."

Dixie laughed as she whirled about, her expressive freckled face at that moment being far more attractive than that of her prettier, younger sister.

"Of course you should," she declared good-naturedly, "and I'm thankful that I have Jimmy-Boy, and here he comes this minute to ask me to give him some bread and molasses."

The door burst open and the small boy ran straight to his little mother, but it was not of bread and molasses that he spoke. "Dixie, dear," he said, and his brown eyes were wide with wonder, "Buddy Ken is in the old barn an' he won't speak to me or nuffin'. I fink he is crying."

[59]

"Mercy, no, not that! A big brave boy like Ken never cries." However, in the heart of the girl who was far too young to be carrying so much burden, there was a sudden anxiety. She had noticed, for several days, that Ken had acted preoccupied, almost troubled. She had not mentioned it, for perhaps he was just figuring how he could sell the apple-crop to the best advantage. Yes, surely that must be all that was the matter. Dixie went on with the polishing. There was just one lid to do and then the task would be finished.

"Run away, Jimmy-Boy," she said in her singing voice. "Play until Dixie is through, and then you shall have your nice bread and molasses."

"Don't want bread; want Buddy Ken to fix my wagon and he won't speak to me. He's crying inside of him, Ken is." At this the small boy burst into tears.

The last rub had been given to the stove, so Dixie washed her hands, and, kneeling, she kissed the small boy as she said: "James Haddington-Allen Martin, I guess it's time to ask you to count your blessings. Now, sir, begin. Blessing one is—" She paused, but she didn't have long to wait. The clouded face brightened and throwing his arms about his "little mother," he cried, "*You!*"

[60]

The girl held him in a close embrace. Then she said: "Carol, dear, please give Jimmy-Boy his ten-o'clock bite while I hunt up Ken. I'm afraid he's worrying about the apples." Carol was glad of anything that would relieve her from the hateful dusting.

Catching her sunbonnet from its place by the door, Dixie went in search of her brother who was her confidant and dearest friend. If he were keeping something secret from her, it would be the first time. Then she smiled as she thought, "Maybe even Ken needs to count his blessings." Singing to cheer herself, she went down the path that led to the old log barn.

"K-e-n! K-e-n! Where are you, brother?" There was no response, and since it would be impossible for the lad to be in the barn and not hear the cheery voice that had called, Dixie's anxiety increased. She entered the wide, front door and glanced about. At first, coming as she did from the dazzling sunshine the girl could not see the boy, who was seated in the farthest, darkest corner. His hands were over his ears, and that was why he had not heard her approach. Truly, he did look the very picture of despair. Instantly Dixie knew that her surmise had been correct. Something had gone wrong about the apples.

[61]

Hurrying to his side, she slipped an arm over his shoulder and laid her cheek on his thick, red-brown hair. "Brother, dear," she said, as she sat beside him on the bench, "here's Dixie, your partner. Please let me carry my share of whatever it is."

The boy reached out and grasped the hand of his sister and held it hard. When he looked up, there were tears trickling down the freckled face that was so like her own. "Did you go to town this morning, Ken?" was the question she asked.

The boy nodded. "Yes," he said, "I went before sun-up. I heard the apple-buyer from Reno would be at the inn to-day, and I wanted to be on hand early. I took along a basket of apples to show, and I thought they were fine, b-but, Dixie, they w-weren't fine at all. W-when I saw the apples from the Valley Ranch, I knew ours were just a twisty little old cull kind. Tom Piggins was there from the V.R., and he said our apples are the sort they feed to their hogs. I didn't stay to show them to the buyer, I can tell you. I just lit out for home, b-but now there won't be any money for you to buy a new stove."

[62]

"I don't need a new stove," Dixie said emphatically. "My goodness me, come to think of it, I wouldn't have a new stove for anything, now that I've spent two hours and twenty-five minutes polishing the old one. It looks so fine. I'm sure it will feel heaps more self-respecting, and I shouldn't wonder if it would bake better, too." Then her eyes brightened with the light of inspiration. "Ken Martin, we'll give it a chance to show what it can do right this very minute. You fetch in that basket of apples you had for a sample, and I'll make an apple pudding, the kind you like so much, and we'll celebrate."

"Celebrate? For what?" Ken looked up curiously. Was there no end to the cheerfulness of this sister of his?

Dixie was groping about in her mind for something over which they might rejoice. "Oh, we'll celebrate because we have a new teacher," she announced triumphantly, and the next thought made her clap her hands joyfully. "Ken Martin, if it's what you'd like to do, I wish you'd go right over to the inn and invite Miss Bayley to lunch."

[63]

Their beautiful mother had always called the noon meal lunch, although Pine Tree Martin could never remember, and had always called it dinner.

Ken rubbed his sleeve over his eyes and looked up eagerly. "Then you really aren't so terribly disappointed about the apples?"

"Disappointed? Goodness, no! I'd feel sort of mean selling that old stove of ours that's been so faithful all these years just for scrap-iron, and, what's more, I feel sure all this is a blessing in disguise." Dixie had risen and was smiling down at her brother, who also rose.

"Say, Dix," he said, "you're as good as a square meal when a fellow's hungry." Then he laughingly added, "But, if not selling the apples is a blessing, it sure certain is well disguised."

"Most things are blessings soon or late," Dixie said. "Now, Ken, you go and tell Miss Bayley we're sort of celebrating, and we'd feel greatly honored if she would come."

[64]

Then into the house Dixie bounced to share her joyous plan with Carol. "Oh, how I do hope teacher will come," that little maid said. "Then we'll be first to have her, and won't I crow over that horrid Jessica Archer though?"

"You'd ought not to feel that way about anybody, Carol, dear," the older girl admonished as she sat on the doorstep and began to pare apples. "If folks are horrid-acting, they are to be pitied, because they can't be happy inside. Now, if you like, you may set the table with the best cloth and china while I make the pudding and put some potatoes in to bake."

The violet-blue eyes of the younger girl were shining. It was a great treat to her to be allowed to open the big old-fashioned cupboard that held the set of china that had been their mother's. When Ophelia had first come to the log cabin, there had been only the thickest and most serviceable kind of ware, but when Pine Tree Martin found what a hardship it was for his wife to use it, he had sent to Reno and had ordered the choicest set they could procure. This was kept carefully locked in the great old cupboard, and used only on rare occasions.

[65]

Jimmy-Boy had been placed in his crib, which was in the lean-to room, where also was the big four-posted bed in which Ken slept. The two little girls chatted happily as they prepared for the great event.

"What if teacher can't come?" Carol paused every now and then to say, and dozens of trips she took to the open door to look up the trail toward the cañon road. At last she gave a triumphant squeal.

"Here comes Ken, and teacher is with him. Oh, goodie, goodie, good!" Carol was pirouetting like a top. "Won't I brag it over Jessica, though!"

Then, as the two drew nearer, the small girl called excitedly, "Dixie Martin, whatever is that thing that Ken's carrying? It's wriggling so he can hardly hold it. Whatever can it be?"

[66]

CHAPTER SEVEN
THE BLESSING UNDISGUISED

The two girls ran out to meet their most welcome guest, the new teacher. Ken, who for the moment had stepped behind the massive trunk of one of the great old pine trees to hide, then appeared, and Carol gave a shout as she said: "Why, Ken Martin, if you haven't got a little pig! Oh-o, don't let it get away. I'm terribly scared of pigs."

No one, looking at the shining, freckled face of the boy, would have dreamed that only an hour before that same face had been the picture of misery.

"It's that blessing in disguise, Dix," Ken said, as he triumphantly held up a rather skinny and very young member of the porcine family.

[67]

"Why, Kentucky Martin, wherever did you get that pig?" the older sister inquired. "I didn't know you had one penny left after you'd bought your high-topped boots."

"I didn't buy him, Dix," Ken declared. "I had him given to me."

Here was indeed an astonishing statement, for pigs were valuable. This one, though, was an unusually skinny-looking specimen. The boy, believing that he had sufficiently aroused the curiosity of the girls, went on to inform them:

"Well, as I was going up toward the inn I heard an awful squealing over in Ira Jenkins's pen, and I ran to see what was the matter. Seems that their old sow had always disliked this little pig, and wouldn't let it nurse with the others, and so Mrs. Jenkins had been keeping it in the house behind the stove; but the blacksmith tripped over it this morning, and he said it would have to go back in the pen where it belonged, even if the mother-sow ate it up, bones and all. Ira had just put it in the pen when I came along, but the old sow had made for it and in another moment the little pig would have been dead, certain-sure. Ira just leaned over the fence doing nothing, and I said, 'Aren't you going to save that little pig's life?' And he answered: 'No. What's the use? It can't live in our house, and it seems like it can't live in its own, so it might as well be dead.' Then he grinned and said, like he thought I wouldn't dare, 'If you can save that little pig, you can have it.'"

Dixie's eyes were wide. "Ken Martin, I hope you didn't get right into that pen where an angry old sow was. Don't you know they will turn on a boy just as quick as anything?"

Ken nodded, and then looked down at his overalls that plainly showed that he had not escaped without a muddying.

"Yes, I know," he said, "but I took a chance, and I'm glad I did, for now we own a pig. I've always wanted one, and, oh, Dix, I'm almost glad we didn't sell the apples." Then, as he held the squealing little creature up to be admired, the boy added, "I've named him already."

Carol sniffed. "I shouldn't think a pig would need a name," she said.

Ken chuckled. "I've named him 'Blessing,' and now if you'll excuse me, Miss Bayley, I'll go and build him a place to live. Carol, will you come along and hold him while I'm putting up a fence for his pen?"

"Me, hold him? I should say not!" and the dainty little girl held back her skirts as though the very thought of touching the creature was contaminating.

"Maybe I can help," Miss Bayley surprised them all by announcing. "I never *did* hold a pig,—we don't have very many of them in New York,—but there's always a first time for everything."

The boy's eyes plainly showed his admiration, and down toward the barn these two went, while the girls returned to the house to put the finishing touches on the lunch. Half an hour later Carol called from the door, and a returning shout from Ken carried the message, "Come on down, first, and see the pen."

Hand in hand Carol and Dixie darted down the path, and how they laughed when they looked over into the very small yard that Ken had fenced off. Too, there was a large box, open at one side, with fresh straw on the bottom, that would make a fine bed.

[70]

The skinny little pig looked up, almost fearfully, at the four laughing faces that were peering over the top rail at him. "After lunch let's get some apples and feed him," Carol suggested.

Suddenly Dixie thought of something. "Why, Ken Martin, we can't feed your little pig apples yet; he's still taking milk."

"That's so," said the boy, snapping his fingers. Then he added: "I say, Dix, couldn't you find the bottle Jimmy-Boy used to have? I can feed him with that, like as not."

"I believe I know just where it is," the little mother said, "but come now or the apple pudding will be done too much." And so, promising the small pig that he would soon return, Ken leaped the fence and they all went up to the cabin.

[71]

A merry lunch it was, and the apple pudding was done to a turn. Indeed, never before had the old stove baked so well, and it seemed to shine with pride. Miss Bayley declared, and she meant it, too, that she could not remember when she had so enjoyed being guest at a luncheon party, and when, at last, she announced that she must go, as there was a letter to be written before the stage came, they all trooped with her to the top of the cañon road.

When they were home again, Dixie declared: "There now, Ken, you said this morning that you couldn't think of anything to celebrate about, and just see what a wonderful day we've had. It's always that way, I do believe. When a person feels gloomy, if he'd just up and prepare to celebrate, even if there's nothing to celebrate about, something will turn up, certain-sure."

"You're right, Dix. You always are," her brother declared warmly. "Two things turned up, the pig and Miss Bayley."

But a harder problem to solve than that of a poor apple-crop was just ahead of brave little Dixie.

[72]

CHAPTER EIGHT
A QUEER BANK

It did seem as though some little imp of mischief was trying to worry poor Dixie Martin. She had been far more sorry about the failure of their apple-crop than she had confessed, for, although the old stove would do for another year or two, the little mother knew that Carol's best dress was actually shabby, and that night, after the small pig had been fed with a bottle, to the great delight of Jimmy-Boy, and after he and Ken were asleep in the lean-to, and Carol in the loft, Dixie sat up in bed and listened, to be sure than no one was awake.

[73]

The light of the full moon streamed in at the small window of the loft, and so she did not need to light the candle. Lifting the corn-husk-filled mattress at one corner, she drew forth an old woolen sock that had belonged to Pine Tree Martin. Nobody knew how the girl, who had inherited so many of his courageous, optimistic qualities, treasured that and every other little thing that had belonged to the man whom she so loved. Indeed, as Carol's admiration had been all for her mother, very much of Dixie's had been for her father, which was not strange, for she had been old enough to see how selfish were the demands of the rather weak, though truly beautiful, woman, and how constant were the willing sacrifices of her father.

The money in the stocking was Dixie's savings for the entire year, and she knew, even before she emptied the few dimes and nickels out upon the counterpane of her bed, that there was nowhere near enough to buy Carol a store dress, and even if there might be enough for material, who was there to make it? Kind old Grandmother Piggins on the Valley Ranch had made them each a dress two years before, the ones that buttoned down the front, but now she was dead, and there was no one to care for them.

[74]

Slowly Dixie counted. There was just two dollars and thirty cents, and Jimmy-Boy ought to have a warm coat before winter, that is, if he were to go to school. When he didn't go, the other three children had to take turns staying at home with him, and when one only went to school two days out of every three, one couldn't make as much headway as one desired, that is, not if one were as ambitious as Dixie. With a sigh that would have been perfectly audible had any one been awake to hear it, the dimes and nickels were replaced, the sock again knotted, and Dixie was about to put it under the mattress when she suddenly held it close to her, and, looking up at the sky, she sobbed under her breath: "Oh, Dad! Dad! You'd know just what I'd ought to do. How I wish you were here to tell me!"

Just then Carol turned over, and, fearing that she might waken, Dixie slipped the precious sock into its hiding-place and climbed back into bed, but not to sleep, for her thoughts kept going over the problem without finding a solution.

[75]

Ever since her father had died, Mr. Clayburn, the kindly banker over at Genoa, had sent Dixie twelve dollars a month, which, he said, was interest on money that her father had left there for his children. The principal, he had assured Ken and Dixie, was invested in good securities that would probably continue to provide for them the princely income of twelve dollars a month.

During the summer it was not hard for Dixie to manage, for Ken raised many things in his garden, but in winter, when there were warm clothes to buy and no garden to help provide, the little mother found it very hard to make ends meet, and now it was October and there was only two dollars and thirty cents in the sock.

"Well," she thought at last with a sigh, "Carol's old dress will have to do, and Jimmy'll just have to stay at home from school when cold weather comes."

It was very late when Dixie Martin closed her eyes in restless slumber, but even then the little imp of mischief was not satisfied, for, when the girl's gold-brown eyes opened wearily, it was on a day when a still greater problem was to confront her.

CHAPTER NINE
THE "CHARITY BARREL"

It was noon of the day following the luncheon party, and as it was the one Sunday of the month on which the Reverend Jonathan Cressly held a religious meeting at Woodford's Inn, the little Martins had been attending the Sunday school.

The text had been, "Little children, love ye one another," but the kindly old man departed in his rather ancient buggy, drawn by a shambling old white horse, with a feeling that his talk had not been entirely successful, for he had heard one little girl, who was very much dressed up, making fun of the Martin girls because they wore dresses that buttoned down the front.

"Those Martin children are certainly a problem in the parish," Mr. Cressly had told the Home Missionary Society in Genoa, and the women had collected clothing that they thought might fit, and had sent a brimming barrel over to the log cabin in Woodford's Cañon. That was soon after the father died, but, to their unutterable amazement, the same driver had brought it back on his cart, saying that Miss Dixie Martin wished him to thank the ladies, as she knew they meant it kindly, and that although she and her sister and brothers weren't needing charity, she was sure there were many families in the mountains that did—the Washoe Indians in the creek-bottom, if no one else.

"Whew-gee!" Lin Crandel, the expressman, had ejaculated. "That red-headed gal stood up like she was the president's darter, she sure did, but it was the purty curly-headed one that spieled the most about how blue-blooded they were. Didn't folks know as they were Haddington-Allens of Kentucky? Whew-gee! I kin tell you I felt like apologizin' for offerin' 'em that barrel."

Of course, after that the ladies of the Home Missionary Society did turn their energies in other directions.

The four little Martins were at home again, and Dixie was setting out a cold dinner, for, true to the teaching of his orthodox mother, Pine Tree Martin had insisted upon one thing, which was that Sunday should be kept holy, and that no work that was not absolutely necessary should be done on that day. Since his wife had never worked very much on any day, this had been no hardship for her.

After the simple meal, Ken said that he was going to walk over to the Valley Ranch, and that they all might come along if they wished. Jimmy-Boy was delighted, for if there was one little pig in their home sty, there were a hundred at the Valley Ranch. Carol liked to go, for Susie Piggins, aged fifteen years, went to a boarding-school in Reno, but came home for the week-ends. Dixie usually enjoyed hearing Sue tell of her experiences, but to-day she said that if the others didn't mind she would like to just stay at home and rest.

[79]

Ken's understanding brown eyes gave one quick glance at his comrade-sister, and noting that she was pale and that she leaned back in the big grandfather's chair as though she were unusually weary, he decided that it would be doing her a kindness to take the other two children away for the afternoon. Little did he dream that the paleness came from long hours awake in the night.

The three had been gone for some time when Dixie was awakened from a light slumber by some one calling: "Whoa, there! Here we are, Dobbin."

Leaping to her feet, though still feeling a little dazed from having so suddenly awakened, Dixie opened the door, to see on the path the kindly banker from Genoa. At once there was panic in the heart of the girl. Why was he coming in the middle of the month, or indeed why was he coming at all? For the past year he had sent the money the first of every month by Ira Jenkins, who did his banking over at Genoa, and was glad, in his gruff way, to do a good turn for his little neighbors, the Martins.

[80]

Samuel Clayburn climbed out of the buggy and smiled at the girl. She invited him to enter the cabin with a dignified little manner that she had inherited from Pine Tree Martin, who had stood as straight and erect as one of the trees that he so admired.

"Won't you be seated, Mr. Clayburn?" Dixie asked, wondering why her knees were shaking so that she could hardly stand.

"I can't stop but two jiffs, little girl, but I thought I'd rather tell you myself than write; seemed like a more humane thing to do, as I am a father myself."

"Oh, Mr. Clayburn," the child leaned forward eagerly. "Has something happened to the money? Is it all gone?"

Dixie was sitting on the very edge of a straight-backed chair, and her folded hands were tightly clenched. Mr. Clayburn was plainly at a loss to know how to begin. He had not supposed it would be so hard to tell a small girl that—

"Little Miss Dixie," he suddenly exclaimed, after having tried in vain to think of some way to lead gradually up to the matter of business upon which he had come, "please don't take what I am going to say too much to heart." Then his kind, florid face brightened as an inspiration came to him. "I have a fine plan," he assured her, "a very fine plan which will make it all right in the end. I am sure of that."

[81]

"In the end, Mr. Clayburn? The end of what?" Poor little Dixie remembered, just then, that that was what had been said when Grandmother Piggins was dying—"It's near the end now."

She gave a little dry sob, and the good man took out his big red handkerchief and mopped his brow. Then, coughing to clear his throat, he began on a new tack. "Dixie, my wife has taken a great liking to little Carol. She saw her last month over at the county fair, and she said then that she'd like to adopt her to grow up twins with our little Sylvia. It's bad for a child to be brought up alone, you know,—makes them selfish,—and we're afraid our little daughter is beginning to be spoiled, and so we've had it in mind for some time to adopt another little girl if we could find a real nice one who needed adopting."

[82]

For a moment the listener sat as one dazed. She could hardly comprehend what the kind man was saying, but, when he paused to mop his brow again, Dixie exclaimed: "Oh, but Mr. Clayburn, I couldn't give up my little sister, Carol. She surely wouldn't want to leave Ken and Jimmy-Boy and me"; but even as she spoke, Dixie feared that she was wrong. Carol would be eager to go, probably, and what right had Dixie to keep her pretty younger sister in a log cabin when she might be living in that fine big white-pillared house in Genoa that was surrounded with a wide lawn and beautiful gardens?

Then it was that Dixie thought of something, and a little of her father's keenness appeared in the thin, freckled face as she said, "Mr. Clayburn, you didn't come all the way from Genoa on a Sunday just to say that, did you?"

[83]

The banker confessed that that had not been his original purpose for making the journey. "You are right, little Dixie," he said; "I came to tell you that there has been a depreciation; that is, the securities in which your father's small principal is invested, are not as valuable as they were, and hereafter your monthly income will only be nine dollars instead of twelve, but, don't you see, dear child," the kind man leaned forward and took her hand, "if Carol comes to live with us, the nine dollars will go even farther than the twelve did with four of you?"

Dixie nodded miserably. Each member of the little brood was infinitely dear to her, and she was so proud of Carol, who looked just like their beautiful mother.

Looking up with tear-brimmed eyes, she said tremulously, "I oughtn't to stand in her way if she wants to go, and more than likely she will. She likes pretty dresses and things that I can't get for her, 'specially now, that there'll only be nine dollars a month."

The heart of Mr. Clayburn was deeply touched and he hastened to say, "Little Miss Dixie, don't you want me to write just once more to your aunt down South?" He arose as he spoke.

There was a flash of pride in the eyes of the small girl. "No," she said. "Never again. We're not going to push ourselves in where we're not wanted."

[84]

"You're right in one way, Dixie," the banker agreed, "but it's my opinion that your aunt doesn't know that you exist. She has never opened even one of the letters. They have been returned just as they were sent."

"Then she won't have the trouble of returning another." The little girl also had risen, and, as the banker started toward the door, she impulsively held out her hand as she said, "Mr. Clayburn, thank you for being so kind,—I mean about Carol,—and if she wants to go to you, shall I send you word by Mr. Jenkins?"

"Yes, yes," the portly gentleman said. Then, as he placed a fatherly hand on the red-brown head of the girl, who somehow seemed smaller than he had remembered her, he added cheerfully: "It isn't as though you won't be able to see your little sister often. You and Ken and the baby can come and have nice visits at our house, and Carol can come here."

[85]

But even to himself this did not ring true. Mrs. Clayburn, who was known as a social climber, had said that if she took Carol, she wished it distinctly understood that Sylvia need have nothing to do with the others, who were so like that impossible man whom the mountain people had called Pine Tree Martin.

Poor Mr. Clayburn held the trembling hand in a firm clasp as he said warmly: "There now, little girl, don't be worrying any more than you can help. You'll be surprised how fine things are going to turn out. Good-by. I'll come after Carol when you say the word."

As soon as the banker had driven out of the dooryard, Dixie threw herself down in the big grandfather's chair and sobbed as though her heart would break, but at last she rose, washed her face, tidied her hair, and began setting the table for supper. The other three would soon be returning, and the little mother of them all would have to be the one to be brave, outwardly at least. But oh, how the heart of her yearned for the father whose strong arms had always been her haven of refuge! But now she, Dixie, must be haven for the other three.

"Here they come," she told herself. "Now we'll talk it over, and Carol may make her choice."

[86]

CHAPTER TEN
CAROL'S CHOICE

When the three children entered the big living-room of the old log cabin, Ken was the first to notice that Dixie had been crying.

"I knew it, I just knew it!" the boy blurted out. "You're sick or something, Dix. That's why you looked so pale, and why you didn't want to go for a walk like you always do Sunday afternoons."

"No, Ken, it isn't that," the oldest girl said. "Get your hats off and come and sit here a while. I want to tell you all something."

Dixie lifted little Jimmy-Boy and held him crushingly close. Then she hid her face among his thick yellow curls, that Ken might not see the rush of tears to her eyes, for she had suddenly thought, "The next thing I know, somebody will offer to take my baby away from me, but, oh, they can't have him, not if I work my fingers to the bone to keep him!"

[87]

Luckily Ken remembered that the pig, three hens, the goat, and Pegasus must be fed before dark, and, as it was dusk, he hastened to the barnyard. Carol had climbed to the loft bedroom to put away her one treasure, a hat with a pretty flower-wreath on it, and so Dixie had time to dry the telltale tears before they returned.

"Fire ahead, Dix," was Ken's boyish way of announcing that he was ready to listen. He whirled a straight-backed chair about and straddled it as he spoke.

Dixie had not planned what she should say. She left it to the inspiration of the moment. What she said was: "Mr. Clayburn has been over while you-all have been away, and he said his wife would like to have Carol go to Genoa and live with them and be a sister to their Sylvia."

[88]

If Dixie had hoped that Carol would say that she would far rather live in the log cabin with them, she was doomed to disappointment, for Carol's pretty face glowed joyfully, and, clapping her hands, she cried: "Oh, Dix, how wonderful that will be! Just think of the pretty clothes I'll have. That old ruffly dress of Jessica Archer's will look like poor folks by the side of the dresses I will wear. Why, Sylvia Clayburn had on a pink-silk dress at the fair. I'd be the happiest girl on earth, Dix, if I could have a silk dress and have Jessica Archer see me wearing it."

Ken had not spoken, but he was watching both of his sisters very closely, and the slow anger of Pine Tree Martin was mounting in his heart.

Suddenly he blurted, "Let her go, Dix, and be glad to get rid of her, if that's all the thanks she's got to give, after the scrimping and going-without you've done to buy her things."

"Don't, Ken, dear," Dixie cried. "Carol's not as old as we are, and—she's different."

"I should hope I *am* different," the younger girl replied, tossing her curls. "I am a Haddington-Allen through and through, my mother often told me so, and you two are—are—"

[89]

"Don't you dare say it!" Ken warned, and Carol, after a quick glance at her brother, thought best not to complete her sentence.

The boy had whirled the chair away and was standing. Looking steadily at the now shrinking younger girl, he declared, "Dix and I are proud, proud, *proud*, that we are children of our father." Then there was a break in his voice that made even Carol ashamed of herself.

"Oh, I don't see why we need be mad about it," she said in a wheedling voice, "and I should think you two would be glad to have me living where I could have nice things and won't have to dust and—"

Again Ken blurted out with, "Yes, you're quite willing Dix should go on doing all the work and bearing all the burden. We'll be well rid of you, I say, and the sooner the better." At that the boy turned and left the house, closing the door with a bang.

The next day Dixie sent word to Mr. Clayburn, and the following Sunday noon, true to his promise, the banker reappeared.

Carol wore her best clothes and had nothing to carry. When it came to the moment of saying good-by, Dixie, to outward appearances her own cheerful self, kissed her little sister tenderly, and Ken said, "So long," not knowing whether he was glad or sorry. Then Carol stooped to kiss little Jimmy-Boy, who suddenly threw his arms about her neck and held her close. "Jimmy loves Carol," he prattled, as he put his dewy mouth up to be kissed.

For one brief moment the little girl hesitated, then, unfastening the clinging baby arms, she ran and climbed into the waiting buggy and sat beside Mr. Clayburn. Then she smiled and waved. Little Jimmy, not in the least understanding what was happening, began to sob and reached out his chubby arms.

Dixie caught him up and held him as she waved his small hand at the disappearing wagon. Then, with a sigh, the little mother turned back into the log cabin, feeling very much as though there had been a death in the family.

To the very last she had hoped that Carol loved them all too much really to leave them; but Ken was calling to her, and so, holding fast to Baby Jim's hand, she went out to the barnyard to see what he wanted.

CHAPTER ELEVEN
PLANNING A WAY OUT

The evening of the day when Carol had ridden away from her log-cabin home to live in the handsome colonial residence of the banker of Genoa, Ken and Dixie sat up later than usual. Ken had a slate on the table in front of him.

"The taxes are twelve dollars a year," he was saying, "so, just as soon as the money comes each month, we must put one dollar in a safe place."

Dixie nodded and then glanced at the tall grandfather clock. It was nine. She wondered if Carol had remembered to say her prayers before she went to bed, and would she miss Dixie's good-night kiss. Perhaps not that very first night. She'd be so excited and interested, everything being so new and strange. Never before had the older girl spent even one night away from any of her little brood. She supposed that she might get used to it in time, sleeping alone in the loft.

[92]

"Dix, you're not paying the least mite of attention to what I am saying." Ken's voice was patient, but he was a little vexed, for he knew that he, who had always been a faithful brother and friend, was being neglected while Dixie was yearning for their vain, selfish sister, Carol.

"I heard what you said, Ken, dear, honestly I did! You were saying it would take two dollars to buy a sack of dry beans, and another two dollars for potatoes that we need right now. That's five dollars out of this month's interest, and there'll be another for extra things like salt and sugar. It doesn't look as though there'd be enough to buy a coat for Jimmy-Boy, does it? And the cold winter will soon be here."

[93]

The brow of the lad was wrinkled, and unconsciously he tapped his pencil on the slate as he thought. Then suddenly he rose with a look of determination that was so like his father's. "Dix," he said, "I'm not going to school any longer. I'm going to work, that's what. I'm fourteen years of age now, and the law lets you stop then."

The girl also had risen, and, placing a hand lovingly on the arm of her brother, she said, "Kenny, you know that your heart's set on going away to school some day to learn how to make roads and bridges and things like that."

Ken nodded. "I know," he said. "Maybe later I can go to school again, but just now we need money."

The lad had been twelve years of age the year that the State road had crossed the Sierra Nevada Mountains. He had been a frequent and fascinated visitor at the camp where the civil engineer lived, and Frederick Edrington, isolated from people of his own kind, had really enjoyed the companionship of the intelligent boy, and had taught him many things, leaving in the heart of the lad an unwavering ambition some day to become a civil engineer.

[94]

When the camp of the road-builders had been moved farther and farther west, Ken had managed to visit his friend until the distance became too great, and at last he had to say good-by to Frederick Edrington, who had been a greater influence for good in the boy's life than either of them at that time realized.

Now and then a letter or a picture postcard had come from the engineer, who had been promoted to a government inspecting-position which took him to many out-of-the-way places. One of Ken's dearest desires was to meet again this friend whom he so admired.

"Don't stop going to school yet, Ken, dear," Dixie was saying. "Let's wait till we get close up to trouble's stone wall, and then, if we can't find an opening in it, we'll turn back and do something else." That had been a favorite saying of Grandmother Piggins. "Trouble ofttimes seems like a stone wall ahead, but when you get right close up to it you find there's an opening with sunshine and gardens just beyond."

Ken whirled about and caught his sister's hands. "I'll make a bargain, Dix," he said. "If you'll promise not to grieve about Carol, I'll promise to keep on going to school until we come to the stone wall and find there isn't an opening."

Dixie smiled. "I ought to be glad," she said, "because Carol is to have so nice a home." Then she added wistfully, "I'm going to be glad, honest I am, just as soon as I get over being lonesome."

Ken turned away and shook the stove. "Girls are queer," was what he was thinking, but it was with unusual tenderness that he kissed his sister good-night.

CHAPTER TWELVE
CAROL'S NEW HOME

It had been a very excited little girl who had driven in between the high stone gate-posts and had realized that the imposing white mansion-like house set far back among fine old trees, and surrounded by wide velvety lawns and gardens, where a few late flowers were still blooming, was to be her future home. Since the little lass was very like her mother, it was not strange that Carol truly believed that she was receiving only that which it was her right to have.

Little Sylvia Clayburn she knew not at all, and Mrs. Clayburn she remembered vaguely as being a very richly dressed woman who had stopped her at the fair to ask whose little girl she might be, and, as usual, Carol's reply had been that she was a Haddington-Allen of Kentucky. Later, when Mrs. Clayburn had heard the story of the four orphans from her husband, she had said that she believed this little Carol would be the right child for them to adopt, since they had decided that their precious Sylvia was being spoiled growing up alone.

Nor were they wrong, for Sylvia, pale, thin, and fretful, indeed was very much spoiled. Whenever she cried, her mother gave her candy, and then, of course, she had no desire for plain, healthful foods.

"Sylvia has such aristocratic taste," the proud mother would say. "She scorns such plebeian food as bread, and will eat nothing but cake."

No wonder that the child of such a mother should be spoiled and sickly.

It was late afternoon when Mr. Clayburn led Carol into the luxuriously furnished library, where Mrs. Clayburn, reclining on a divan, propped up with many silken pillows, was reading aloud to a small girl who was dressed in the pale pink silk that had so aroused Carol's envy and admiration.

[98]

Languidly the woman lifted her eyes and closed the book when the newcomer approached. "Wife, here is little Carol who has come to pay us a good long visit, I hope," the kind man said. Then to his own little daughter he added, "Sylvia, won't you come and shake hands with your new sister?"

Mrs. Clayburn protested. "Samuel," she said, "haven't I told you time and again that hand-shaking is effete, obsolete? It is not done now in the best families."

Carol, wishing at once to impress Mrs. Clayburn with the fact that she, at least, was of a "best family," was making a graceful curtsy, and Sylvia, having received a prompting push from her mother, did likewise.

"As you wish, my dear," said Mr. Clayburn, smiling as though he were much amused.

"As long as this little lady is welcomed into our hearts, I'll not be a stickler as to what outward form is observed," he thought. Then to Sylvia he said, "Miggins, trot along upstairs and show your new sister where to put her bonnet and things."

[99]

"I don't want to," the small girl said, again seating herself by the divan. "I want Mother to read to me."

"Of course you needn't go if you don't want to," Mrs. Clayburn told her.

Then she said to her husband: "Ring for Fanchon. Poor Sylvia is thin enough as it is without wearing herself out needlessly climbing up and down that long flight of stairs. We really ought to have a lift installed. They are now putting them in the homes of the b—"

But Mr. Clayburn had gone. Good-natured as he was, he was becoming extremely tired of hearing what was done in the best families.

[100]

There was a button in each room in the house, which, when touched, rang a bell in the kitchen, and the indicator informed the maid where her presence was desired, and so it was that a moment later a buxom young woman in black and white appeared in the library door. Her rosy countenance suggested that she was Irish, and in fact, when the banker's wife had engaged her, the maid's name had been Norah, but since the best families were employing French maids whenever they could be procured, the name had been changed to Fanchon. However, Mrs. Clayburn had warned her not to speak within the hearing of a guest, as her delightful brogue could never be mistaken.

Carol followed the silent Fanchon up the long flight of stairs that seemed velvety soft, and into a large, beautifully furnished chamber where there were twin beds. The small girl clasped her hands in delight. This, to her thought, was the kind of home in which she belonged. How happy she was going to be there!

"Will you be after changing yer dress now, colleen?" the Irish maid said pleasantly. "This here's the one as the mistress said ye were to be wearin' for dinner to-night." As she spoke she took from a closet one of Sylvia's dresses. "That child took a dislikin' to it," the maid went on to inform the small listener, "and not once would she be puttin' it on. Ye're in luck, colleen, changing this quick from gingham to red silk."

[101]

The "blue-blooded" little girl looked with horror at the dress. It *was* silk, but how she had always hated bright red. She actually drew herself up as she said: "I don't wish to wear it. I wish a blue silk dress."

Now it happened that Mrs. Clayburn, on second thought, had decided to climb the stairs and see just how the little orphan liked her new surroundings, and so, holding the hand of Sylvia, she had just entered the room unseen as this most ungrateful remark was being uttered.

"Indeed, Miss Martin?" she said in a tone of mingled iciness and sarcasm. "What can you, a mere charity orphan, be thinking of to tell what you wish to wear? You ought to be humbly grateful that you are being taken out of that tumble-down log cabin and permitted to live in a house as handsome as any belonging to the best families."

[102]

For one brief moment a spark of Martin pride flamed up in the heart of the small girl. Their log cabin was not tumble-down. Only that summer an artist from the East had said that it was the most picturesque home that he had seen in the whole State of Nevada. That was when the crimson rambler had been a riot of bloom.

Wisely she said nothing, but meekly permitted the maid to put on the hated red dress.

The swish of the silk was something after all.

Poor little Carol had not started out well, and she was to find that, although she was living in a rose-garden, it was not one without thorns.

[103]

CHAPTER THIRTEEN
CAROL IN DISGRACE

The dinner was one of many courses, and there were two very formal guests, and, to Mr. Clayburn's mortification, as well as Carol's, the hostess, wishing to impress the fashionable Mr. and Mrs. Jarvis Burrell, from Reno, with her philanthropic generosity, told in detail the story of Carol's life, beginning when her mother was a stranded actress in the year of the big strike over at Silver City.

[104]

The kind man glanced often at the small girl whose face was becoming as scarlet as a peony. He well knew that he would be publicly rebuked by his wife if he remonstrated or attempted to change the conversation, and yet were it not better that he should bear the brunt of it than this mere child who had been invited to come to their home? But, before he had time to decide just how best to intervene, Mrs. Clayburn had reached a point in her narrative which necessitated a description of the father, who, she informed them, had been a no-account rancher, called by the mountaineers "Pine Tree Martin." She said no more, for the small girl, with flaming eyes, had risen so suddenly that her chair fell back with a crash. "'Tisn't so!" she cried, her small hands clenched. "'Tisn't so, at all!" She had whirled to face the visitors. "He was the kindest, best father there ever was to Dixie, Ken, Baby Jim, and me." Then, bursting into tears, she ran from the room and groped her way blindly up-stairs and into the room to which Fanchon had first taken her.

She was pulling at the buttons in the back of her red-silk dress when she heard a step outside the door. It was Mr. Clayburn who entered.

"Carol," he said, placing a kindly hand on the curly head, "don't be hurt, little girl. Mrs. Clayburn is thoughtless, but she can't be really as cruel as she seems. You sit here in this comfortable chair by the fire and I'll have the rest of your dinner sent up to you."

[105]

He started away, but he turned back to say, "You were right, though, little Carol. I knew your father well, and he was the finest and most upright of men. Any girl might be proud to be his daughter."

Then he left the child alone in the room that was but dimly lighted, and as she sat there waiting the coming of Fanchon, for the very first time in her life she felt a real love and loyalty for that man whom the banker had just praised. How kind he had always been, and how gentle. If—if this cruel, wicked, Mrs. Clayburn was "best families," she'd rather, oh, a hundred times rather, have her own dear, good father, whatever he was.

Fanchon entered, bearing a tray, and placed it on a low table. "Poor little colleen," she said with understanding sympathy. "I'm not after envyin' you much, and that's the truth. I can be leavin' any hour I choose, as I'd like to, after next pay-day; but I'm supposin' you'll have to stay here to the end of time."

[106]

Then she went away, and Carol sat staring into the fire, thinking of what she had just heard. Did she have to stay there for ever and ever? Ken wouldn't want her back, and, after all, did she want to go back? Maybe things would be better after that night, and it was something to be able to wear silk; even red silk was better than gingham. The dessert was a delicious concoction, and Carol, as she ate it, decided that perhaps she had been partly to blame that things had started out so all wrong. Just then Fanchon reappeared and she was leading Sylvia by the hand. That little maid looked with big-eyed wonder at the newcomer.

"You're a very bad, bold girl; that's what my mother says you are; and I'm not going to speak to you again till you say you're sorry; and I shall hate you always." Then she closed her thin lips tight and did not speak again while the buxom Irish maid was undressing her. Later Fanchon unfastened the buttons of the red-silk dress, helped Carol to prepare for bed, and then turned out the light.

There had been nothing said about prayers. Carol had never in all her short life gone to bed until after prayers had been said. When Pine Tree Martin lived, he had gathered his children about him in the warm kitchen and had led in the evening prayer, and had read to them from the big Bible. Ken did the reading now, in memory of his father.

When Carol was sure that Sylvia was asleep, she crept from bed, and, kneeling in the moonlight, she said the little bedtime prayer that Dixie had taught her, and then asked a blessing for each of the three who were in the log-cabin home over in the mountains.

Then she crawled back into bed, feeling somewhat comforted, but she never, just never, could forgive Mrs. Clayburn; she was sure of that. Suddenly she sat up, thinking. What was it that Dixie had taught her? Never to let the sun go down on her wrath. But the sun had gone down, and the moon was up. Oh, what ought she to do? After all, maybe she had seemed ungrateful. Dixie wouldn't want her to go to sleep without asking to be forgiven.

Creeping out of bed, she stole down the wide, velvet-soft stairway, holding her long white nightgown in one hand, while she grasped the banister with the other. The guests were just departing when they looked up and saw the small girl descending. Mrs. Clayburn was horrified.

"Go back to bed this instant, you bad, bold child!" she commanded, and so, too frightened to speak, Carol did turn and go back, to sob softly into her pillow until, at last, just from weariness, she fell asleep.

So ended the first day of Carol's life in the home of one of the "very best families."

CHAPTER FOURTEEN
THE LITTLE RUNAWAY

The next morning Sylvia was unusually fretful, and little wonder, for she had had two helpings of the rich, creamy dessert the night before, and would not eat the wholesome breakfast which was served to her in bed.

Carol was told to remain in her room that morning as a punishment for the manner in which she had misbehaved the night before. This message was brought with her breakfast by Fanchon. To the surprise of the maid, the small girl was up and had on her own old dress that buttoned down the front.

"Oh, I just wanted to put it on," the child said, when the kindly maid expressed her surprise.

[110]

"Poor little colleen, I guess ye're homesick, and I wouldn't wonder at it if you are," was what Fanchon was thinking, but aloud she made no comment, as the pale-blue eyes of her little mistress were watching her from the bed where she sat propped among downy pillows.

All the time that Carol sat at the low table eating her mush and milk, she, too, was wondering if she could be homesick. Almost unconsciously her eyes roamed over the creamy net curtains and rose-silk draperies, at the bird's-eye maple furniture, and at the wide window-seat heaped with rosy cushions.

Then her thoughts wandered to the little loft bedroom which she and Dixie always shared together. There was one small window, with a turkey-red curtain, a very old-fashioned chest of drawers, and in one corner sat her doll, Peggotty Ann. Of course she was too old now to play with dolls, for would she not be nine the very next month?

She glanced at the little brass bed in which she had slept. It was covered with creamy net, lined with rose-colored silk. Spread over the four-posted bed at home there was a many-colored piece-quilt that her grandmother had made when she was a bride.

[111]

Somehow that loft-room seemed more homey after all. Fanchon had come to take the trays. She asked Carol if she wished to put on one of Sylvia's pretty morning-dresses.

"No thank you, not yet," the child replied. She walked over to the window and looked out. It was a gray, gloomy day. If she were looking out of a window at home, she would probably see Ken digging around somewhere in the garden and whistling. What a jolly whistler Ken was!

Just then Sylvia, unable to longer remain unnoticed, said fretfully, "Carol Martin, I was just falling asleep, and you made so much noise you woke me right up, and my mother said I was to sleep all of this morning because I am sickly."

Carol felt that this was very unjust, for a little mouse could not have been more quiet. She sat down in a chair by the window, trying hard not to cry. Sylvia spoke again, "Well, as long as I can't sleep, you may bring me my best doll, and be sure you don't drop her."

[112]

Carol looked in the direction indicated and saw a beautiful French doll that was nearly as big as she was. "Oh, what a beauty," she exclaimed.

Very carefully she lifted it and took it to the little girl in the bed. Then she turned away and was far across the room when a shrill scream from Sylvia was followed by a crash. Sylvia had let the doll slip from the bed.

"You did it, you horrid beggar-girl," she cried, "and now my beautiful doll is broken."

The door burst open and Mrs. Clayburn appeared. She had hastily thrown on a velvet lounging-robe and her hair was down her back.

"Mother," Sylvia fairly screamed, "she made me drop my doll."

Again the just wrath of a Martin was in the heart of Carol. "You *know* you're fibbing!" she said almost scornfully. "I'm not going to stay here another moment. I'm not! I'm not! I'm going right home to-day where folks live who are honest, and who l-love me, and I'm not going to say I'm grateful 'cause you brought me here. I'm not! I hate you. I just hate you both!"

[113]

Dashing to the closet before the astonished woman could realize what was happening, the girl snatched her best hat from a hook and ran from the room.

The bell for Fanchon sounded through the halls. "Stop that child before she gets out of this house. Then lock her up in the coal-room," was the imperatively given command.

"Yes, ma'am. Which way was she after goin', ma'am?" the maid lingered to inquire.

"How can I tell, stupid! She can't unlock the front door, so she is probably there this minute, trying to get out."

Mrs. Clayburn was right. That was where the Irish maid found her, but instead of taking her to the dark, windowless basement-room, Fanchon quickly unlocked the front door and set her free.

"Poor little darlint," the maid thought, as she glanced anxiously up the long flight of stairs to be sure that she was unobserved, "it's me as is wishin' I had a log-cabin home in the mountains I could run away to."

[114]

Mrs. Clayburn, at an upper window, saw the small figure flying across the lawn. She went at once to the telephone and called up the bank.

"Samuel, have that child caught and brought back here at once. She's got to beg my pardon and be properly punished before she can leave this house."

But the banker was busy, and he failed to send any one to search for the little runaway, and so, though Mrs. Clayburn watched and waited, at noon the culprit had not been returned to her. Several hours later her husband called to say that he was going into the country on business and would not be home to dinner.

"Poor little Carol," he thought as he started driving toward the mountains, "she probably has tried to walk home, but her little legs will tire out long before she gets there, and no one living along the way except the Washoe Indians." Mr. Clayburn hastened the pace of his horse as he thought of this. Meanwhile Carol, on leaving the home of the banker, had slipped unobserved through side-streets until she came to a highway on the outskirts, which she believed led in the direction of her log-cabin home.

[115]

She had been to Genoa but once before, and that was when she was six years of age, and though she knew that she must follow one of the side-roads toward the mountains, she was not sure which one to take.

On and on she trudged. The houses were very far apart now, and at last there were none at all. The child looked very small indeed as she crossed the desert-like stretch of sandy waste where only sagebrush and a few twisted trees were growing.

At last she reached a crossing, and to her joy, a sign-post informed her that Woodford's was but six miles away over in the mountains. At least it was a comfort to know that she was going in the right direction. The pine trees grew bigger and denser and the road began to ascend.

[116]

The child's feet were very tired, and, at last, she was so weary that she felt that she just could not take another step, and so she sank down on a boulder to rest. How silent it was, save for the moaning of the gentle breezes in the pines. The only living thing that she saw was a great wide-winged vulture that was swinging around overhead in circles. Never in her life had the child felt so alone in the world, but she was not afraid. The children of Pine Tree Martin had never learned fear.

"I must hurry on," she thought, as she again arose and trudged bravely up the rough mountain road. With feet that would lag, however eager she might be to go on, she slowly climbed, but, with five miles still ahead, the small girl realized that she could walk no farther. Sinking to the ground, she curled up under a pine tree and began to sob softly.

Suddenly she sat up alert, listening. She had heard the pounding of a horse's feet around the curve that she had just passed. Some one was coming!

[117]

She hid behind the trunk of a tree that she might see without being seen, and then watched and waited. Soon a horse and rider appeared. After one glance the small girl, with a glad cry, leaped out into the road. It was Tom Piggins riding on a big dappled work-horse. He had been to Genoa on an errand for his father, and was returning to the Valley Ranch. Never before had Carol been so glad to see any one.

Running out into the road, she waved and shouted, "Tom! Tom! Please give me a ride!"

"Why, Carry Martin, what you doin' here?" For once the small girl did not resent being called by that much-hated name. The long, lank boy continued: "Ken was over to our place last night, and he was sayin' as how you'd been adopted by a rich banker. He said he was sort of glad of it, you being so selfish and hard to live with, but Dixie, she's been sniffling 'round ever since you left, and the little kid keeps askin', 'Where's Carol? Jimmy wants Carol.'"

Upon hearing this, the small girl sobbed afresh.

"Oh, Tom," she cried, "I don't want to be adopted. Please, please take me home."

The blunt boy was nevertheless kind, and so he helped the small girl up on the big horse in front of him, and, as they rode along, Carol told the whole story to sympathetic ears.

"Gee-crickets!" the boy exclaimed admiringly. "I'm certain glad you had some of your pa's spunk." Then he added hopefully, "Maybe you're goin' to change, and get to be more like Dixie. Ken'll like you heaps better if you do."

Carol said nothing, but in her heart she resolved that she would try to be so much like Dixie that folks wouldn't be able to tell them apart.

It was noon when Tom helped the little girl to the ground in Woodford's Cañon, and, after having thanked him, she started walking slowly down the trail toward the log cabin, for a dreadful thought had come to her. What if she wouldn't be welcome. What if Ken should say, "You left our home and now you can stay away."

The window nearest the trail was open, and Carol thought she would look in before going to the door.

CHAPTER FIFTEEN
A HAPPY REUNION

Within the cabin the three children sat about the table, eating their midday meal. Carol at the window heard Ken say: "Dix, this is the second day that you haven't eaten one bite. If you get sick, how on earth'll Baby Jim and I get along?"

The girl turned from the table and began to sob. "I'm sorry, Ken," she said, "truly I am, but I don't know that I'll ever be able to eat again unless Carol comes home."

"Well, I sort o' wish she'd come, too," Ken declared, blinking very hard.

There was a sudden warm glow in the heart of the little listener. After all, she would be welcome. Even Ken wanted her! With a glad cry she ran in the open door and threw her arms about her sister. Then she pounced upon Ken and kissed him.

"I'm home," she cried, "and please, please let me stay forever and ever."

Baby Jim was clamoring for attention, and he was caught in a crushing hug while he waved his spoon and uttered joyous little squeals, although he did not understand Carol's homecoming any more than he had her departure only the day before.

After a time, in which tears and laughter blended, Carol cried, "Dixie, I'm 'most starved with that long walk and not eating much breakfast. I'm so glad you've got fried potatoes and baked beans."

"I'm hungry, too, now that I take notice of it," the older girl said, her freckled face beaming.

"Well, I thought I'd had enough, but I guess I could take another helping," Ken declared. And so they all sat down, and a merry meal it was.

[121]

Oh, how much nicer her own home was, Carol thought, where even Baby Jim could talk if he wished and not be told that only grown-ups should converse at table. Carol didn't tell all that had happened. In fact, she didn't seem to wish to speak of her recent experience. She inquired with interest about the well-being of the pig and the three hens as though she had been away a year.

Then she asked what had happened at school that day. None of them had attended. They hadn't had the heart to do anything, but on the morrow all of them would go.

After the dishes were done, Carol climbed to the loft. For some reason that she could not explain to herself, she wanted to see her old doll. She hadn't played with it for a year, not since Jessica Archer had made fun of her and called her a baby for playing with a doll.

How cosy the loft bedroom seemed, the small girl thought as she reached the top of the ladder. Those turkey-red curtains, with the sunlight shining through them, were very cheerful looking. Peggotty Ann was probably the most surprised and the happiest doll in the whole State of Nevada, when, a moment later, she was caught up and kissed by her little mistress.

[122]

Ken entered the kitchen, and, going to the table where Dixie sat sorting the mending, he said very softly, that the girl in the loft might not hear: "Dix, something'll have to be done, now that Carol's back. We can't make ends meet on nine dollars a month, and one to be laid aside for taxes."

Dixie looked up brightly. "There's still two dollars and thirty cents in the sock, Ken," she said, "and we haven't reached trouble's stone wall yet."

"Dix," the boy declared admiringly, "you're a brick!" Then he added, with a mischievous grin, "and I don't mean because you're red-headed, either."

A moment later when Carol, with her doll in her arms, looked out of the small window in the loft, she saw Ken digging in the garden and heard him whistling, and, for the first time in her young life, she realized something of the contentment and joy contained in that one word, "home."

Being very, very tired, after an almost sleepless night and a long walk, the small girl curled up on the husk-filled bed to rest, her doll held close. Soon she was asleep, and so she did not hear a horse and buggy stop at the door. In fact, she never knew that Mr. Clayburn had called, but Dixie knew, and what that kind man told brought joy to the heart of the little mother.

The banker said that he was glad to inform her that he had succeeded that very morning in loaning her father's small principal in a way that would bring fifteen dollars a month interest.

He did not tell her that he had loaned the money to himself, as he knew that no one else would pay so high a rate of interest, and he was determined that the wolf should be kept from the door of the four little orphans who were too proud to accept charity.

When he was gone, Dixie ran out into the garden.

"Ken! Ken!" she called, and the boy thought that never before had he seen her face so aglow. "We've reached trouble's stone wall, and there *was* an opening through and on the other side is a garden that's all sunshine."

CHAPTER SIXTEEN
A JOYOUS DIXIE

The next morning Miss Bayley's glance wandered often to the corner of the room in the old log schoolhouse where sat the four little Martins. She wondered why they all looked so beamingly happy. Little did she dream of the exciting events of the day before. Not only had the small prodigal returned, but their monthly income had been increased, and no longer need the little mother scheme, plan, and contrive just to make ends meet. Little Jimmy-Boy's much-needed warm coat now could be purchased as soon as the money came, and that would be at least two weeks before the really cold weather set in. In fact, there were years when November was as pleasant as October, and where, in all the world, could one find more beautiful autumn weather than in Nevada?

When Dixie, as usual, led the opening song, her voice rang out with lilting joyousness, and when she stood up to read, Miss Bayley was charmed with the expression with which she interpreted the little story. In fact, so pleased was she that she forgot to stop Dixie at the end of the second page, as was the custom, but permitted her to read the entire story of "The Three Bears." It delighted her to note how Dixie's voice changed when Papa Bear or the Baby Bear spoke.

Then, when the little reader had finished, the teacher exclaimed with real appreciation: "Dixie, you read that splendidly! You surely have a gift."

Then it was that she recalled that the mother of the Martin children had been an actress, and a very audible sniff also reminded her of the fact that she was praising some one who was not a daughter of the board of education.

[126]

The sniff had come from the front seat, center, and the sniffer was, of course, the haughty little Jessica Archer. That maiden had risen, and, with a toss of her corn-colored curls, she announced, "Miss Sperry, our last teacher, said I was the best reader in this school, and my father said yesterday that she was the best teacher we'd ever had in Woodford's."

Miss Bayley was indignant, and yet, if she wished to remain, she must be politic, and now that she was so interested in the Martins, more than ever did she want to stay.

"You read very nicely, Jessica," she told the irate little maid, "especially when you are thoroughly acquainted with the text. You may now read the entire story of 'Henny Penny.'"

Somewhat mollified, Jessica Archer read the tale which she knew by heart, forwards or backwards, with more expression than was her wont. She did not intend to have those no-account Martins win more praise than was given to her.

With an inward sigh Miss Bayley assured Jessica that she had never before heard her read so well, which indeed was true, and then she called upon Ken to do an oral problem in arithmetic.

[127]

At recess, when the other children had trooped out of doors to play, Dixie remained, and Miss Bayley, who was writing on the board, turned to find a pair of eager eyes watching.

"Did you want to speak to me, Dixie, dear?" she inquired.

"Yes, ma'am, Miss Bayley, please, if 'twouldn't be interrupting too much. I want to ask advice about something that's very secret."

The teacher smiled. She believed that she was at last to learn the cause of the inward glow that radiated from the thin, freckled face of the older Martin girl, who was sometimes called "homely."

But the secret something was destined not to be told, for just then Jessica Archer, who had missed Dixie from the playground, entered the schoolroom in search of her. Not that she desired the companionship of a Martin, but she did not wish to give Dixie an opportunity to be alone with the teacher.

Miss Bayley frowned, and very softly she said: "Dear, can't you come over to my cabin after school to-night? I very much want to have a real heart-to-heart visit with you."

[128]

"Oh, teacher, Miss Bayley, I'd love to. You can't think how I'd love to!" was the eagerly given reply.

Jessica Archer could not possibly have heard, and so it was merely a coincidence which prompted her to say, "Miss Bayley, my mother said I was to tell you to come home with me after school to-night and have supper at our house."

"Thank you, dear," Miss Bayley replied, "I am sorry that I cannot accept. Please thank your mother for me, and tell her that I had already made another engagement."

The young teacher was rebellious. Her free time, surely, was her own, and she determined that she would do with it as she pleased.

[129]

Dixie was about to protest that she could come any other day just as well, but there was an expression in her dear teacher's eyes that silenced her. Then as the clock marked the hour of ten, Miss Bayley rang a bell which ended recess and recalled the small pupils to their lessons. Jessica Archer, with another toss of her corn-yellow curls, seated herself, feeling that she was not being treated with the respect that was due the daughter of a sheep-king. She was suspicious, and that was why she lingered so long after school, rubbing imaginary marks from her reader, washing off the top of her desk with unusual care, and all this time, while the teacher was preparing examples for the following day, Dixie Martin sat on the bench outside of the little log schoolhouse, happily waiting.

At last the teacher's patience reached the breaking-point. Looking up from her work, she found the pale-blue eyes of the daughter of the board of education watching her.

"Jessica Archer," she exclaimed, and the degree of exasperation she felt sounded in her voice, "will you kindly tell me why you are remaining? The afternoon session ended at least fifteen minutes ago. You will please leave at once, and do not remain after school-hours again without asking my permission and explaining your reason for wishing to do so."

Jessica's expression was decidedly impudent. "There's that Dixie Martin staying after school."

[130]

The teacher's eyes narrowed. "She is not in the schoolhouse. I have no control over all the big out-of-doors. What is more," and this took moral courage, "Dixie is waiting for me at my request. Now take your books and go!"

Miss Bayley had never before been so angry at a pupil, for she believed, and truly, that she was being spied upon by the small daughter of Mrs. Sethibald Archer.

Jessica did depart, but she did not go home at once. Having reached a clump of low-growing pines near the inn, she hid among them to await the return of Miss Bayley to her small cabin home. At last she saw her coming, and with her was the hated Dixie Martin, and, what was even more shocking, Miss Bayley was swinging the little girl by the hand and skipping; yes, she was actually skipping in a way that no self-respecting teacher had ever done before.

Jessica remained in her place of hiding until she was sure that Dixie was going in the cabin with the teacher. Then, when she believed that she was unobserved, she crept but, keeping hidden as best she could behind the sagebrush, until she reached the trail that led down to her valley home.

[131]

Bursting into her mother's room, she began to sob. Mrs. Sethibald Archer at that moment was struggling to write a speech, and a very large dictionary lay open on the table at her side.

Her real reason for having invited Miss Bayley to supper that night had been to have the assistance of the teacher in preparing the paper which she was to read on the day following in Genoa. Once before Miss Bayley had given invaluable assistance, and the ladies had greatly praised Mrs. Sethibald on her clear and lucid exposition of the subject. Just what that meant, the speaker of the day had not known, but she was convinced that it was praise, and she was desirous of doing equally well on the morrow.

"Do stop crying," the weary mother now remonstrated, "and tell me where is Miss Bayley? I didn't see her coming down the trail with you just now."

[132]

"She—she wouldn't come, Ma," Jessica sobbed afresh. "She—she treats me awful mean. She says that horrid Dixie Martin is the smartest girl in the school. She says she can read better'n I can. I told her you wanted her to come to supper to-night, and she said she had another engagement, and—and, ma, it wasn't so. She just had Dixie Martin go home with her, that's all, for I hid and saw, and she didn't act ladylike neither, ma; she skipped!"

Mrs. Sethibald Archer arose, and the expression in her eyes was not pleasant to see. "There's your pa coming into the barnyard this very minute," she said. "Run right out, darling of my heart, and tell him not to unhitch. Tell him I'm wishing him to drive me over to the inn. We'll see whether or not my requests are to be set aside like this."

Jessica ran out to deliver the message, which was really a command, and Sethibald Archer understood it as such. Then, returning, the child asked eagerly: "Ma, I want to go along."

"Of course you may go. This thing's going to be settled this very day. I'm not going to have any upstart of a teacher refuse my hospitality when I offer it. Indeed not."

[133]

CHAPTER SEVENTEEN
A DEFIANT TEACHER

When Dixie entered the pleasant living-room of the little log cabin near the inn, she clasped her hands, and her eyes glowed with appreciation as she looked about.

"Oh, teacher, Miss Bayley," she breathed rapturously, "you've got books, haven't you? I never did see so many books all in one room. Oh, please, may I touch them?"

Then it was that the young teacher remembered that the little girl had said that "Oliver Twist" and "Pilgrim's Progress" were the only books that she had, and an almanac.

[134]

"Poor little story-hungry girl," she thought, as she removed her hat and turned toward the child. "Of course you may touch them, dear. I'm going to make us some hot chocolate to drink, and you may browse around all that you wish. Choose any book that you like and I will help you read it. One of my reasons for asking you here to-day, Dixie, was to suggest that once or twice a week you come with me and let me tutor you in advanced reading. Then you can take the book home and give the same instruction to your brother, Ken. There is no reason why you two children, who are so unusually gifted, should be held back by one of little natural intelligence."

Then Miss Bayley entered the lean-to which was also her kitchen, and humming to herself to endeavor to erase from her memory the unpleasant conflict with Jessica Archer, she filled the tiny teakettle, lighted the oil-stove, and prepared a few dainty sandwiches.

When she re-entered the living-room, her small guest sat on the window-seat, one long, spidery leg curled under her, and she held two books. The gold-brown eyes seemed to have sunshine in their depths as they looked up.

[135]

"Oh, teacher, Miss Bayley," she piped, "it was so hard to choose. It's like when the spring flowers are in blossom and the valley-meadow is all blue and gold with them. There are so many, and they are all so lovely it's hard to tell which ones to pick. I guess, though, that these two would be nice. This one says 'Little Women' on the cover, but that wouldn't interest Ken so much, it being all about girls, but this one would, for, in the picture, there is a boat wrecked and animals swimming to the shore. I'm sure boys would like it."

Miss Bayley nodded, beaming her pleasure. "You will like that one, too. My brother, Tim, and I read 'Swiss Family Robinson' through seven times when we were your age and Ken's."

Skipping over to the long, home-made bookshelf, the child replaced "Little Women," and held lovingly the volume of her choice.

Then a cheerful humming in the kitchen announced that the teakettle was beginning to boil, and Miss Bayley went thither to complete preparations for the lunch.

While they were eating it, the young woman, who was little more than a girl herself, having graduated from a normal school when she was hardly twenty years of age,—and this was her first school,—smiled across at her small guest as she said: "Dearie, at recess you wanted to tell me something. What was it?"

[136]

"I'm going to tell you all about us, Miss Bayley."

Dixie's thin, freckled face became suddenly serious. "I'm going to tell you all about us, Miss Bayley," she began, "then I guess you'll better understand."

And so the little mother of the Martins told to a most sympathetic and interested listener the drama which had recently been enacted in their log-cabin home.

"And, oh, teacher, Miss Bayley," the child said, "I never, never could have come to school again if my little sister had stayed away. She's all the sister I've got to love. I couldn't give up Ken or Baby Jim either, but—but I guess a girl needs another girl in a special way that boys can't understand, don't you, teacher?"

The young woman nodded emphatically, and there were tears close to her eyes. What a cruel, hard experience these children had been going through, and all alone.

[137]

"I do, indeed, Dixie," she said. "There are so many tasks and pleasures and little confidences that only girls can share with each other, but I am glad that everything happened just as it did, for now Carol knows that her own home is best and she will be more content."

But Dixie looked a bit troubled, and the young woman asked: "Dear, what is it? Was there something else that you wished to say?"

"Yes, teacher, Miss Bayley, it's this. Next month is Carol's birthday, and, oh, if only I could give her a blue silk dress I'd be the happiest! She loves pretty things and she's never had anything silk." Then eagerly, anxiously, "Miss Bayley, could I get a silk dress for two dollars and thirty cents?"

The young teacher hesitated not at all. "Of course you can, dear girl. That is, you can get the blue silk by the yard and then you can make the dress."

[138]

The freckled face that at first had brightened, looked doleful again. The child shook her head as she said: "I couldn't, teacher. I don't know anything about how to put on patterns. Grandma Piggins did, and she made us the gingham dresses, but she made them button in front, and Carol wants buttons in the back."

"And so she shall have them, dear. Of course you can't use a pattern yet, but I will show you how." Then, before the small girl could express her gratitude, the young teacher exclaimed: "I'll tell you what we'll do, little Miss Martin. To-morrow will be Saturday, and you and I will go to Genoa on the nine-o'clock stage, shall we? Then you may choose the silk and a pattern. I have some lace in my trunk that will do nicely for trimming. How would you like that?"

"Oh, teacher, Miss Bayley, I'd love it! I've never been to Genoa but once." Sudden tears in the child's eyes assured Miss Bayley that the once had been a sad occasion, as indeed it had been, for with her father she and Ken had gone to select a coffin for their beautiful mother.

Desiring to change the thought of her little guest, Miss Bayley asked, "What color do you like best, Dixie?"

"I like the first green that comes on the trees down by the creek in spring. It's like a fairy color with silver on it," the little girl said.

Miss Bayley nodded. "That would make a pretty silk dress," she remarked, "but I'd like you to have a cashmere dress, the same gold-brown as your eyes."

"Me? Oh, I don't need a new dress, Miss Bayley. I don't mind buttons down the front the way Carol does."

The young teacher laughed, saying, as she rose to clear the table, "We shall see what we shall see."

Dixie was about to assist when the sound of wheels attracted her attention. "Oh, teacher, Miss Bayley,"—the child seemed actually frightened,—"something dreadful must have happened. Here come all the Archers."

There was a sudden firmness about Josephine Bayley's pretty mouth, and an expression in her eyes that seemed to say, "Let them come."

CHAPTER EIGHTEEN
THE SHEEP-KING DICTATES

Miss Bayley opened the door when she heard an imperative rap thereon.

"Oh, good-afternoon, Mrs. Archer and Mr. Archer," she said graciously. "Come in, won't you, and Jessica? You are all acquainted with my little friend, Dixie Martin, and so introductions will not be necessary. Won't you be seated? This is my most comfortable chair, Mrs. Archer, and Jessica, you will find room over on the window-seat by Dixie."

The wife of the sheep-king sat down, but held herself rigidly erect. "Miss Bayley," she said, "didn't you get an invitation to come to our house to supper?"

"Why, yes, Mrs. Archer, but did not Jessica tell you that although I appreciated your thoughtfulness, I could not accept to-day, as I had another engagement?" Miss Bayley was calm, and completely mistress of the situation.

The older woman sneered. "Engagement?" she repeated sarcastically. "How could you have any engagements in these here parts that couldn't be set aside when I need your services?"

Miss Bayley's eyebrows lifted, ever so slightly. "I did not understand that you needed me," she said. "I thought that you wished to contribute to my pleasure by inviting me to supper."

Mrs. Archer's manner changed. "Well, so I did in a way, and if you'll go back with us now," she said, "I'll call it all right." She knew that unless Miss Bayley did help her, she would be unable to read a paper before the Woman's Club in Genoa on the next day.

For one brief moment Josephine Bayley hesitated. Should she defy this woman and declare her right to independence at least as far as her free time was concerned? A second thought reminded her that this would be unwise, if she wished to remain in the mountain country; and now, more than ever, she did wish to remain, that she might help little Dixie Martin, if for no other reason.

[142]

That small girl had risen, and in the pause she said shyly: "Teacher, Miss Bayley, I must be going. Baby Jim is like to be missing me by now."

"Very well, dear." The teacher also rose and walked to the door which she opened, and then said, loud enough for the listeners to hear without effort: "Dixie, be ready to-morrow morning at half-past eight. You would better come up here, dear, and then the stage will not need to stop on the cañon road."

Then, closing the door and turning back into the room, she added pleasantly: "I suppose, Mrs. Archer, that you wish me to prepare a paper for you. If that is true, I will get my hat and coat and accompany you."

Her manner, in spite of the graciousness of her words and tone, was defiant, and when she returned from her screened bedroom, she found Mr. Archer, his hands behind him, pacing up and down the living-room.

"Look a-here, Miss Bayley," he blurted out, "my wife and me aren't at all satisfied with your actions. It's us chiefly that supports this school and pays your salary."

[143]

The teacher's eyebrows lifted questioningly. "Indeed?" she said. "I thought this was a public school in the Genoa district."

Mr. Archer was obliged to confess that, in one way, it was. "But it's my taxes, mostly, that pays your salary," he contended.

"When taxes are paid into the county treasury, the money is no longer yours," Miss Bayley told him. "It belongs to the people to be spent for the best interest of the entire community."

The young teacher's manner was quiet, but she spoke as one who knew.

Mrs. Archer, unable to longer remain silent, burst forth with: "You might as well understand, once for all, that Mr. Sethibald Archer is boss of this here school, and what he says goes. Mr. Samuel Clayburn, the banker, he as is head of the board of education over in Genoa, told Mr.

Archer that as long as everything went along all right, he'd not interfere with my husband's management of this here school district."

[144]

The ponderous woman rose, and her expression was one of triumph. Mr. Archer nodded his agreement. "That's just what the Honorable Clayburn said, and so, if you're wanting to remain in this here school, you'd better not be setting those no-account Martin children up over our Jessica. Now, are you coming with us, Miss Bayley?"

To their unconcealed amazement, the young teacher mutinied.

"No," she said quietly, "I am not. I consider my free time my own to do with as I wish, and I do not wish to go anywhere this evening."

A dull red suffused the face of Mr. Sethibald Archer. "Miss Bayley," he sputtered, "this here term ends the middle of December. You can pack up your baggage and be ready to leave the day after."

"Very well, Mr. Archer," was the astonishing reply, "if you are still in authority when that time arrives, I shall do as you request."

[145]

When the three were again in their buggy and on their way down the valley road, the irate man exclaimed: "Such impudence! If I'm in authority by the middle of December, she'll leave. Huh, she'll leave all right! Who else in these here parts has brains enough to be governing board of a public school?"

Mrs. Archer, being a wise wife, smoothed his ruffled feelings by remarking: "Nobody, of course. You're the brainiest man anywhere this side of Genoa." Then she added, with a sigh, "I'll have to give up reading that paper to-morrow, and you'll have to drive over and tell 'em I was took sick or something. If I was you, I'd stop in at the bank while you're in Genoa, and clinch the matter about dismissin' that upstart of a Miss Bayley."

"That's just what I'll do!" Mr. Archer agreed, as he drove into his barnyard.

They had forgotten that on the next day the teacher and Dixie Martin were also going to Genoa.

[146]

CHAPTER NINETEEN
DIXIE GOES SHOPPING

Dixie was awake on the eventful Saturday morning as soon as the first bird-note was heard underneath the wide-spreading eaves. Quietly she slipped from bed, hoping not to awaken the little curly-headed sleeper at her side, but, just as she was buttoning up her best gingham dress, Carol opened dazed blue eyes and looked about.

"Why, Dixie Martin, what for are you up so early?" was the puzzled query, but almost instantly the little girl remembered, and at once she began to climb out of bed.

"Oh, I know," she prattled, "this is the day that you go to Genoa with Miss Bayley, and I am to be 'little mother' to Baby Jim and Ken."

[147]

In another moment the arms of the older girl were about her, and the flushed cheeks were being kissed as Dixie exclaimed, "Carol, it's so nice of you not to mind my going and leaving you at home, but some day, I'm just sure, it will be your turn to go and see the shops, and— and everything."

There was joy in the heart of Dixie as she descended the ladder that led from their loft bedroom. How Carol had changed! Just one short month ago she would have sulked if Dixie were to be given some pleasure that she had not been asked to share, but to-day the small girl was actually getting up hours earlier than usual, that she might be a real help in the little home, and that Dixie need not be all tired out before starting on her wonderful journey. But, early as these two little maids were astir, Ken was ahead of them, and, just as the potatoes and bacon were sizzling for breakfast, in he came with a pail of milk.

"Girls," he cried jubilantly, twirling his cap so dexterously that it caught on the hook by the door, just as he wished it to do, "something's happened. Something jolly! Guess what."

[148]

The sisters looked interested but did not venture a guess.

"Blessing is weaned!" was the astonishing announcement. "He wriggled out of his pen in the night I guess. I was awful panicky at first, thinkin' like as not he was lost, but where d'you think I found him? In the shed, eating apples."

"Well, I'm glad," Carol remarked as she continued with her task, "we won't have to bother any more about feeding him with a bottle."

Dixie sighed, "I was hoping you'd say my cat had come back. She's been gone three weeks if it's a day."

Ken laughed as he turned the milk through a sieve. "Cats always come back, sis," he said encouragingly. Then, for a moment, he was silent as he plunged his face into a deep basin of cool water from the pump, but later, when he was rubbing vigorously with a rough towel, he winked one eye at Carol as he added: "Even if Topsy never comes back, it's small loss. The world is full of cats." He said it to tease, for well he knew his sister's devotion to that particular black cat. The expected retort came:

[149]

"Why, Ken Martin, how can you say that, when you know there's only one Topsy cat? You might as well say that if Baby Jim went away, it wouldn't matter, 'cause the world is full of babies."

Carol pretended to be indignant. "Dixie, how can you speak of cats and our baby all in one breath?"

A small voice arose in the next room, and the little mother flew thitherward, to return a moment later with a sleepy, flushed little four-year-old, who was covered with a long pink-flannel nightie. His golden curls were towsled, and when the little maid had seated herself and cuddled him on her lap, he beamed around at them all, but looked up into the face that was bending over him with his sweetest smile. Then, lifting his warm little hand, he patted her freckled cheek as he prattled, "Jimmy-Boy loves Dixie."

Almost convulsively the girl held him close. "Oh, Baby Jim," she said, "I'm awfully sorry I said that about cats, for even if the world is full of babies, after all, there's only just one."

An hour later Carol looked at the clock. "You'd better hurry, Dix," she said. "You wouldn't want to miss the stage."

And hurry the little maid did, and at eight o'clock promptly she set off up the cañon trail with a song singing in her heart, and with feet that could hardly be kept from dancing.

Josephine Bayley was just finishing her breakfast when a tap came upon her door. With the girlish skip which had so shocked prim little Miss Archer, she went to open it, and, as she had supposed, she found Dixie, her freckled face aglow, standing outside.

She was wearing a very pretty leghorn hat wreathed with daisies.

"Why, Dixie, how nice you look!" the young woman exclaimed. "Come in, dear. We can see the stage when it comes up the valley road. What a pretty hat you have."

The girl flushed. "'Tisn't mine, teacher," she confessed. "It belongs to Carol, but she just made me wear it." Then she added in a burst of confidence: "Carol's changed a lot since she went away to be 'dopted. Before that she never would let me even put this hat on in front of the mirror, let alone wear it outdoors, but this morning, when I was putting on my old hat that got caught in the rain last spring and sort of limped, she came right up and took it away, and then, before I knew what she was up to, she slipped back of me and put her treasure-hat right on my head, and when I said something might happen to it, she said, 'All right, let it,' but that she wasn't going to have her big sister go to town in a hat that looked as though Biddy-hen had used it for a nest."

There were sudden tears in the eyes of the little girl. "Oh, teacher," she confided, "I did think that I always loved Carol as much as ever I could, but I'm loving her more every day, and Ken, too. He said last night, 'Gee, sis. I'm glad now Carol went away to be 'dopted, for I'm so glad she came back.'"

"She is a dear, sweet girl," Miss Bayley said, "and it was nice for her to want you to wear the hat which she so treasures, but I'm sure that nothing will happen to it, for there isn't a cloud in the blue, blue sky, and we're not expecting whirlwinds to carry it away."

While they talked, Miss Bayley washed the few dishes and then Dixie helped her spread the bed in the screened-in porch, which was still a joy to the girl who had lived her twenty years in crowded New York.

Just as the last little pat was given to the pillow, a distant rumbling was heard, and Dixie ran to the front window of the cabin and looked down the valley road. "It's coming, teacher, Miss Bayley. The stage is 'most here!"

Josephine Bayley felt as though she were a girl again, a very young girl. Dixie's excitement was contagious. Donning her hat and jacket, and taking her shopping-bag, which had room in it for all the things they were going to purchase, she caught the little girl by the hand, and, though her feet longed to skip, they thought it best to walk demurely, for the innkeeper's wife, Mrs. Enterprise Twiggly, had appeared to greet any newcomers that might have arrived to stay at the inn, and well did Miss Bayley know that she expected schoolteachers to appear morosely dignified.

[153]

Mr. Hiram Tressler, the driver of the stage, was a very old man, having driven that route more years than Mr. Enterprise Twiggly could remember. He had been born and brought up in those parts, but his unwavering good nature and optimism had kept him young-looking, and his life out-of-doors had made him, as he himself said, "as hard as a pine-knot."

"All aboard, them that's comin' aboard!" he called from his high seat. Then, noting that the new teacher, whom he had brought up from Reno but a month before, was about to embark with him, he added, "Miss Bayley, wouldn't you an' little Dixie Martin like to sit up front?"

[154]

The young girl looked up into the face of her companion so eagerly that the teacher gave a laughing response that she was sure they would be glad to accept the invitation. The passengers inside the coach looked like traveling salesmen, with much baggage stowed about them, and they seemed much more desirous of sleeping than they did of admiring the majestic scenery through which they were to pass. One did waken when the stage started with a jolt, but soon dozed again.

Little Dixie, wedged in between Miss Bayley and the stage-driver, looked up beamingly at first one and then the other. "Traveling's real exciting, isn't it?" she said at last, when they were well under way.

Josephine Bayley nodded. Was it amusing or was it tragic, she was wondering, that this little midget, small for her twelve years, had never been out of Woodford's but once before, and that once to help select a coffin. Josephine Bayley resolved that this day should be so brimmed with happy hours that the little girl would have no time to recall the sad memory of that other journey to Genoa.

They were turning down the rough, rugged cañon road that was deep in the shadow of great old pines, when Ken, Carol, and Baby Jim leaped from behind the massive trunks where they had been hiding, and shouted, waving their handkerchiefs, "Good-by, Dixie! Good-by, teacher!" Then Baby Jim's shrill, excited voice floated down the cañon after them, "Bring me some candy!"

What a happy light there was in the gold-brown eyes that were lifted to the teacher, as the little girl said: "I hoped they'd all come. I'm so glad they wanted to!"

Josephine Bayley held the thin hand of the child in a close clasp, and she was thinking: "Lucky little girl! How I wish I had some one to care whether I come or go! Brother Tim is all I have in this wide world, and we are so far apart." Then, remembering that this was to be Dixie's day, the teacher chatted about things that would interest her little comrade, and two hours later Mr. Hiram Tressler sang out, "There's Genoa's church-steeple." Then, with evident pride, "Teacher, did ye ever see any buildin' go up much higher'n that?"

Miss Josephine Bayley, late of New York, had to confess that she had seen steeples a mite higher. She wondered what the stage-driver would think if his route led by the Woolworth building, but how glad, glad she was that it didn't!

Ten minutes later the stage-driver drew rein. "Here we are now. That there's the dry-goods emporium, teacher. I'll pick you up again, right on this very spot, prompt at five o'clock. So long!" Then the stage rumbled away, and Dixie, clinging to the teacher's hand, entered the store, her heart beating like a trip-hammer.

There was silk, silk everywhere about her, and how glad she was that two dollars and thirty cents would buy enough for a birthday dress for Carol.

CHAPTER TWENTY
DIXIE BUYS A SILK DRESS

Josephine Bayley smiled down at the little girl as she felt the clinging fingers tighten. "Oh, teacher," the child whispered rapturously, "I didn't suppose there was so much silk anywhere in all the world. It's like rainbows, isn't it?" They were standing at the counter, waiting for a pleasant-faced little woman to come to them.

"May we see the different shades of blue silk?" Josephine Bayley asked, when at last the clerk turned toward them.

"Oh-ee, how Carol would love that one," Dixie said as she pointed to a blue, the color of a June-morning sky. The small girl did not think to ask the price. Teacher had said that two dollars and thirty cents would be enough, and Dixie doubted this not at all.

[158]

A pattern was selected, one with ruffles, for nothing was to be omitted that the heart of the little sister had been set upon, and then sufficient silk was measured off. Miss Bayley, having had a moment's opportunity to speak alone with the clerk, had asked her not to mention the price. Turning back, she saw little Dixie smoothing the silk as reverently as though it were almost too beautiful to be touched, and yet there was no thought of envy in her heart. Two dollars and thirty cents could buy but one silk dress, and that one should be for Carol.

While the parcel was being wrapped, Dixie looked about. Suddenly she caught the teacher's hand and drew her down the aisle. "Look there," she whispered as she lifted glowing eyes. "That's the silvery green I was telling you about, Miss Bayley. Isn't it like the very first leaves on the willow trees down in the creek-bottom?"

[159]

The young woman nodded. "It is just lovely, dear," was all that she said, but she thought much more. Then, when the saleswoman returned, Dixie drew forth the old-fashioned purse that had been her mother's and counted out the money, which was in dimes and nickels. There were so many of them that it looked like quite a fortune heaped upon the counter in front of her. The little girl did not dream that the silk for Carol's dress had cost five dollars.

"Now, dear," Miss Bayley smiled down at her, "let's go over to the book department. I want to get a more modern arithmetic than the one that I found in the school." While the young teacher was examining mathematical books, Dixie, with a little half-suppressed cry of joy, skipped toward a table spread with attractively-covered juveniles, and so absorbed was she a moment later that Miss Bayley found the opportunity she desired to slip back to the silk counter and order a pattern of the pale-green that in one light shimmered like silver.

Had Dixie noticed the shape of the package that the teacher carried when they left the store, she might have thought it rather soft and bulky for a book about mathematics, but there were so many things to see and admire that she noticed it not at all.

[160]

It was noon, and to the little girl from the mountains the main street of the village seemed thronged. Again she clung to her teacher's hand as they made their way toward the café, over which hung the most alluring sign.

"Oh, teacher, Miss Bayley, are we going in here?" It was hard for the child to believe that she was actually going to have lunch in a place so sparkling with mirrors and lights.

But it was really true, for Miss Bayley was leading her to a little table in one corner that was just for two.

Then when the orders had been given, the small girl, wide-eyed, looked all about her. "There's going to be music," she whispered. "It's over behind those plants." She had seen two violinists in a palm-sheltered corner, and even as she spoke the first sweet strain was heard. Miss Bayley watched the sensitive, expressive face of the little girl and wondered how any one could call her homely.

[161]

It was the first time Dixie had ever heard the music of a violin, and when the last note had died away she lifted eyes that looked as though they had seen a vision. "Miss Bayley," she said, "some time I want to play like that."

And just then the teacher, looking ahead through the years, seemed to see a beautiful, willowy young girl dressed in soft, shimmering green, with red-gold hair glowing beneath the lights, playing a violin, while a vast multitude of people listened breathlessly. Was it a prophecy?

[162]

CHAPTER TWENTY-ONE
DIXIE VISITS A FRIEND

They were again on the street, and the noon throng had vanished. As it was still too early for the afternoon shoppers to arrive, the town seemed to be taking a midday siesta. Dixie wondered where they were going, but said nothing until they turned a corner, when she uttered an exclamation of joy. "Oh, teacher, Miss Bayley," she exclaimed. "There's the bank. How I'd perfectly love to go in and see kind Mr. Clayburn." Then, looking up anxiously. "Would it 'sturb him too much, do you suppose?"

Miss Bayley had a secret desire to see the head of the board of education of the Genoa district, and so she replied, "We can at least inquire, and if Mr. Clayburn is not busy, he may see us for a few moments."

[163]

The banker had just returned from his lunch, and was in his handsomely appointed private office. He was never too busy to see a friend, he told little Dixie, when, wondering-eyed, she had followed the uniformed bank-messenger into the marble-walled room.

"This is our new teacher, Miss Bayley," the child said, not knowing the right form of introduction.

The kind face of the man lighted. Holding out his hand, he exclaimed, "Miss Bayley, this is truly a pleasure, and right now let me say that I sincerely regret not having visited your little school before this, but, since your arrival, I have been more than ever confined to the bank during school-hours. However, I shall endeavor to visit your district regularly after the first of January."

They had seated themselves at the banker's invitation, and Josephine Bayley said quietly, "I shall not be the teacher at Woodford's school in January, Mr. Clayburn."

[164]

There was real regret in the face of the listener. "Why, Miss Bayley, I am sorry to hear that. Has something happened to recall you to New York? I remember you wrote that you would gladly stay one year with us in our wild mountain country." Then he smiled as he asked, "Have you found it too wild?"

The young teacher also smiled, but she said seriously: "No, indeed! I love the West! I felt smothered in that city of walled-in cañons, where the sweep of the wind is never felt. I glory in your rugged mountains. I forget that life holds much that is petty when I look at them, especially at night when they are outlined against the sky, and even the stars are much nearer here. In New York heaven seems farther away."

"But, my dear girl," the banker said, "If you like it here so very much, why desert us?"

"It is because I have been dismissed by the local board of education." If there was a twinkle in the brown eyes of the speaker, Mr. Clayburn did not notice it. He tapped upon his desk with the pencil he held, and a frown gathered between his eyes.

[165]

"Miss Bayley," he said after a thoughtful moment, "I alone am at fault. I should not have entrusted to a man without education the power to engage and dismiss a teacher." Then, looking up inquiringly, "Which one of the three have you offended?"

"All of them, I think," was the reply. "The little girl is indignant because I have to acknowledge that the Martin children are brighter pupils, the mother feels that she has a personal grievance because I will not devote my free time, whenever she wishes, to preparing papers for her to read at your women's club, as her own compositions, while the father considers me insubordinate because I have declared my independence."

"Good for you, Miss Bayley!" was the rather astonishing exclamation. The banker looked his approval. Then, rising, he held out his hand. "Don't begin to pack your trunk, and, as I said before, the first of the year I will make regular visits to the district schools. Let me know if you need new books or anything else to help your work along."

When they were again on the street, Miss Bayley caught the hand of the small girl and said: "Dixie, come with me! We're going to the movies to celebrate."

[166]

CHAPTER TWENTY-TWO
TEACHER REVOLUTIONIZES

Surprising things happened the following Monday morning in the little log schoolhouse. After leaving the theater on the Saturday previous, Miss Bayley, who had been told by the one having authority to procure whatever she might need for her little classes, had returned with Dixie to the book department of the emporium, and had purchased several graded readers from the first to the eighth. The light of a new resolve shone in her eyes as she called upon Dixie Martin to lead in the Good-Morning song.

When this was done, Miss Bayley looked about her at her little straggling group of mountain pupils and made a startling announcement.

[167]

"Girls and boys," she said brightly, "I have decided to change the old régime, which means that we are going to desert the former way of doing things and start in on a new. To begin with, I am going to give you all an examination in reading and place you in the grades where I believe you belong."

Jessica Archer was on her feet in an instant, saying: "My pa wouldn't let you do that. He says nothin' is ever to be done diff'rent in this here school unless he tells the teacher to do it."

"Kindly be seated, Jessica, and hereafter do not speak without first raising your hand and receiving permission to do so." The teacher's tone was firm, and, although the little "sheep-princess" pouted and looked her defiance, she said no more just then.

"I have here," Josephine Bayley continued, "eight new graded readers, that are very attractively illustrated. I will begin with the first, and you may each read one of the little stories; then we will progress to the second, and so on, and, when you have reached the book which is too difficult for you, we will know exactly in which grade you belong. Does this method seem fair to you? Ira Jenkins, what do you think?"

[168]

The long, lank, overgrown son of the burly blacksmith flushed to the roots of his hair, but he managed to uncurl his ungainly length from the much-carved desk that was too small for him, and say stutteringly: "Yes'm, Miss Bayley. Seems like 'tis to me. I should say 'twas fair enough."

"Do any of you, except Jessica Archer, object to being regraded according to your ability to read?" There was no dissenting voice, and so the first book was handed to Dixie Martin, who, with an amused smile, read the tiny story that told the adventures of a pussy-cat. When the book had been passed from pupil to pupil, it was found that even those simple words had been too difficult for the two little children of Mr. Archer's Mexican overseer, and so Franciscito and Mercedes were classed as "first readers."

The six-year-old twins of the trapper, Sage Brush Mullet, poor, forlorn little Maggie and Millie, stopped at the second.

[169]

Jessica Archer did well enough in the third, but could not read many of the words in the new fourth, and was so graded. With her was Carol Martin, but to the very evident indignation of the little daughter of Mr. Sethibald Archer, Dixie, Ken, and Ira Jenkins were placed above her.

Each was asked to read one of the last three stories in the fifth book. Ken and Dixie hesitated not at all, but Ira did stumble over the longer words, and the first story in the sixth proved quite beyond him, and so he was placed there.

Ken, although two years older than his sister, had a more mathematical mind, and found the seventh reader rather difficult, but Dixie reached the last, and was declared by the teacher to be in the eighth grade.

Miss Bayley purposely avoided looking in the direction of the irate little girl in the much-be-ruffled dress as she said: "You are now each placed in the grade where you should be, and I am sure that we shall in the future make real progress." Then, glancing at the clock, she smilingly added: "Ten already, and time for recess. Dixie, you may collect the new books please, and Ken, will you lead the line to the playground?"

[170]

But Jessica Archer did not wait to go out with the others. Catching her hat from its hook on the wall, she darted out, and when, fifteen minutes later, Miss Bayley rang the bell, recalling the pupils to their lessons, she was not at all surprised to find that the rebellious little "sheep-princess" was not among them.

Miss Bayley was not long kept in doubt as to what the absence of Jessica Archer meant. Having decided to carry her new method of grading through all the subjects,—reading, writing, and arithmetic,—the teacher had sent Ira Jenkins and Ken to the board to work out rather advanced sums, when the sound of hurrying wheels was heard without, and a moment later the short, stocky Mr. Sethibald Archer burst into the room, his face flushed, his small gimlet-like eyes blinking very fast.

[171]

"Say, Miss Bayley," he blurted out, waiving the formality of a greeting, "what's this here my gal's been tellin' me 'bout you upsettin' methods which I started and makin' out she's a numskull alongside of those—those no-account Martins? I'll not have it, I tell you," he blustered. "I'm governin' board of this here school, and things have got to be done as I say, or you can pack and leave this here locality on to-morrow mornin's stage. D'ye hear?"

Miss Bayley did not take advantage of his pause to defend her action, and, still further angered by her calm, he went on, his high-pitched voice growing louder, if that were possible. "I'd like to know where from you got your authority,—*you*, an upstart teacher we don't know nothin' about. Who was it told you to spend money that's not yours buying new books that we don't need for this here school?"

[172]

So indignant had been the self-important little man, and so loud his voice, that he had not heard the arrival of a horse and buggy without, nor was he aware that another listener had stopped in the doorway to await the end of the tirade. When the speaker paused to take a breath, the newcomer stepped into the school-room, saying in a voice, the calm, even tones of which did not betray the just anger that he felt: "Mr. Archer, may I answer the question you have just put to Miss Bayley? I, Samuel Clayburn, head of the governing board of education in this district, gave our teacher full authority to purchase whatever she believed was needed to further the interests of this little district school, and I am indeed glad to find that she is now introducing progressive methods." Then he added, in a pleasanter tone, for it was hard for the portly banker to be unkindly severe: "Mr. Archer, I regret that the delivery of mail in the mountain sections is so dilatory, otherwise you would have known by now that I have decided to devote more of my time to the schools in the outlying districts, and so will no longer require your aid. I will bid you good-morning."

The stocky, florid man was clenching and unclenching his hands, and almost bursting with indignation. When the quiet voice ceased speaking, he blurted out with: "It's an outrage, that's what it is! A cooked-up scheme of this here new teacher's to oust me from a place that's rightfully mine. But I'll get even. I'll take my darter out of this here school. Come along, Jessie, I won't have you pizened by no such corruptin' influence."

With a toss of her curls, the little girl flounced out of the door, closely following her irate father, and they were soon heard to drive away.

"Miss Bayley," the banker said, "I regret this most unfortunate incident. Last Saturday, immediately after your departure from the bank, I wrote Mr. Archer that I would no longer need his services, but the stage probably has not as yet passed his place. Realizing that something of this very nature might occur when he did receive the letter, I decided to drive over, knowing that otherwise you would have to bear alone the brunt of his wrath."

"Thank you," Josephine Bayley said simply. "I am indeed sorry to have been the cause of this unpleasantness, but really, Mr. Clayburn, I do believe that the other pupils can now have a much better chance."

The banker nodded, "I am sure of it," he said, as he smiled about at the solemn faces.

"My pupils," Miss Bayley said to them, "this gentleman is Mr. Samuel Clayburn, of the board of education, and he it is who made us a gift of those attractive new readers that have pleased you all so much."

Carol and Dixie arose at once, and the others shyly and stragglingly followed. Then curtsying, as Miss Bayley had taught them to do when she introduced a visitor, in a faltering chorus they piped, "Good-morning, Mr. Clayburn." But it was Dixie who thought to add, "And thank you for the books."

"You are very welcome, and I'm sure you'll make good use of them," was the genial reply. Then, turning again to the girl-teacher, he added: "I hope no further unpleasantness will result from this, Miss Bayley, but if there does, report to me at once. You can telephone to me from the inn."

Later, as he was driving down the pine-shaded cañon road, the good man was thinking, "How I do wish my Sylvia could attend this mountain school. She seems to be making very little headway with her French governess. If only she could live awhile the simple, healthful life that the little Martins are living, how much good it would do her."

CHAPTER TWENTY-THREE
THE RETURN OF TOPSY

"Dixie Martin, come quick if you want to see something. Oh-ee! It's something you've been wanting for weeks and weeks."

It was Carol who called. The small curly-headed girl was hanging out clothes in the sunny yard, back of the log cabin, while the older sister stood on a box beside a washtub in the shade of a spreading pine tree.

Hearing the excited voice of her little sister calling to her, Dixie hastily wrung out the pair of patched blue rompers that she was washing, and, with soapy suds glistening on her hands, she ran around the house, wondering what she was to see.

To her great joy, coming across the garden toward them was no less a creature than her long-strayed and much-loved cat, Topsy.

[176]

With a cry of delight, Dixie wiped the suds from her hands on her blue all-over apron, and rushing at the rather thin and rusty-looking cat, she caught it up in her arms and kissed it on the nose, eyes, and even on the paws.

"Oh, you dearest, darlingest, belovedest!" she exclaimed. "Wherever have you been? You look like a reg'lar tramp cat, and no wonder,—your coat hasn't been sleeked for three weeks if it's a day. Didn't you love your Dixie any more, that you ran away and wouldn't come back? You don't know how lonesome I've been."

The little girl's face was burrowed in the soft black hair. The pussy-cat purred its contentment when its little mistress sat on a stump near by to cuddle it in her lap, but suddenly Topsy flipped up an ear and sat erect, as though she had just thought of something. Then, before the astonished girls could guess what it was all about, away the cat darted toward an old abandoned shed down near the apple-orchard, soon reappearing with a very small something in its mouth.

[177]

The older girl had turned back to the washtub, but another exclamation as excited as the first brought her whirling about.

"Dix Martin, Topsy's done gone and had kittens. Oh-ee, do look! Isn't it a little beauty? It's black, like its mamma, but its spots are white."

Topsy, holding her tail proudly erect, placed the wee pussy at Dixie's feet, then looked up in a manner that seemed to say, "There now, what do you think of that for a baby?"

Dixie lifted the soft cuddly little thing, and was about to tell the happy mother that it was indeed a darling, when, with a queer little short meow, the cat again turned and trotted off toward the shed, to soon reappear with another wee pussy, but this one was as white as the driven snow.

"Oh-h!" the two girls breathed a long sigh of admiration, for never had there been a lovelier pussy, they were sure. Just then Ken, with an ax over his shoulder, appeared from the mountain-trail, whither he had been to cut wood for their winter fires.

"What you-all got there?" he called. And when he saw that they were beckoning excitedly, he threw his axe to the ground and ran toward them.

"Gee whiz! Aren't they beauts?" the boy exclaimed with genuine admiration. "They're 'most as handsome as my little pig," he added teasingly.

"Why, Ken Martin, little pigs aren't warm and soft and cuddly, nor baby goats, either," Carol began, when Dixie interrupted, the light of inspiration in her thin, freckled face.

"Oh, Caroly, you've always wished you had a white pussy, and so you may have this one all for your very own, and Ken can have the other."

"Me?" the boy exclaimed wide-eyed. "I don't want a cat. They're pets for girls."

"Well, maybe that's so. Girls like cuddly things." Then, to the mother puss, Dixie said: "Well, Topsy-cat, we're ever so glad that you have such nice babies, and won't Jimmy-Boy be pleased when he wakes up, but now I must get back to my work, for this is wash-day. I want to get through as soon as ever I can, for something—oh, so interesting!—is going to happen this very afternoon. I am to go up to teacher's to have a lesson."

Dixie did not say what the lesson was to be, but she glanced at her sister and thought, "If Carol only knew that I am to have a lesson in making her a blue-silk dress, wouldn't she be the happiest girl that ever was?"

The younger girl had no desire to accompany Dixie to Miss Bayley's cabin. The very word "lesson" did not appeal to her on a glorious Saturday. After taking the kittens back to the shed and making them a softer bed, the girls finished the washing; then at two o'clock they donned their best gingham dresses and started out together, but soon parted, as Carol was going to the Valley Ranch to visit Sue Piggins, to hear what had happened during the week at the girls' boarding-school over in Reno, which Sue attended.

CHAPTER TWENTY-FOUR
DIXIE'S LESSON IN DRESSMAKING

Miss Josephine Bayley was anticipating with real pleasure the coming of the little girl who was to have her first lesson in dressmaking.

The door of the small cabin stood welcomingly open, for it was one of those wonderful, balmy days known as Indian summer, and in Nevada they seem lovelier than elsewhere.

"See these beautiful ruddy leaves that I found this morning, Dixie, dear," said the young teacher, who stood at the center-table arranging them, as the small girl appeared in the doorway. "I climbed a little lost trail, or, it was almost lost, it was so overgrown with tangled vines and scraggly dwarf pines."

[181]

The great bowl of flaming-leaved branches was placed in one corner of the room, the table swept clear of books and magazines, and then the paper pattern was opened while Josephine Bayley continued, smiling across at her little visitor: "Dixie, how I wish that trails could talk. I'd love to know whose feet trod it so many times that a path was beaten there. Perhaps you have heard, have you, dear?"

Dixie shook her red-gold head. "Not 'zactly heard, Miss Bayley," she replied, "but most likely 'twas the year of the big strike over at Silver City. My dad said that over-night, almost, these lonely, silent mountains were swarmed with men from everywhere, and they climbed all about with their pickaxes, hunting for other veins, but they didn't find them. Maybe it's selfish, but I'm glad, glad they didn't."

"So am I, Dixie," the girl-teacher agreed, "for they would have dug ugly holes in these mountains and cut down the wonderful old pines. I would rather have nature at its wildest for my home than a castle of glistening white marble surrounded with artificial parks, however beautiful."

[182]

"Oh, teacher, so would I." The small girl had drawn close to the table, and her gold-brown eyes looked as though they were seeing a vision. "Miss Bayley," she said, "I keep remembering. I can't forget it. That violin music, I mean. And this morning, early, when I was up before the others, out under the pines, getting ready to do the washing, the sun came up over old Piney Peak, and it was just like a fairy shower of gold. Then a lark sang, and a little breeze stirred in the pine trees. Teacher, Miss Bayley, I think I could play it on a violin, if I had one."

"Little Dixie Martin, you shall have one! You shall have a violin!" the young woman said, deeply touched. Then she added: "I only wish that I knew how to give you lessons, but where there's a will, there's a way. That is a true saying, dear, and you and I will keep watching for the way. Now, little ladykins, if you will stand up very straight and tall, I'd like to see if this pattern hangs well. I'm going to pin it on you, if you don't mind, to get an idea of what kind of dress it will make."

[183]

Miss Bayley did not tell that her real reason for wishing to pin on the pattern was to discover how much larger she would have to cut one before making a certain piece of shimmery green silk into a dress for Dixie.

When the pattern was on, the girl-teacher made many penciled notes on a bit of brown paper. "There, now," she exclaimed, "we'll cut out the material."

Dixie, watching, suddenly put one hand on her heart, as though to still its too-rapid beating. "Oh, teacher," she said in a little awed voice, "this is a wonderful minute, when we're really going to begin to make a blue-silk dress for Carol." Then she added almost wistfully: "How I do hope that dear old Grandmother Piggins knows that you are helping us. Before she died she sent for me and she said, 'Dixie, dear, I'm glad to go, but I'm praying that somebody will be sent to take my place with you.'"

Then impulsively the child cuddled close to the girl-teacher and looked up with love shining in her eyes. "Miss Bayley, you are the answer to Grandmother Piggins's prayer."

[184]

Kneeling, the young woman held the little girl in a close embrace, as she said in a voice that trembled: "Dixie, I have wandered far, and have lost the simple faith, but, oh, what it means to me to know that I, even I, have been found worthy to be used as an answer to prayer!"

Then rising, she merrily added, "Now thread a needle, little Miss Seamstress, and sew these two edges together."

Sitting in a low rocker, by a sunny open window, Dixie took painstaking little stitches, almost measuring each one, but when her girl-teacher noticed that, she laughingly said: "You needn't be so careful, dear. The big thing in basting is to have the notches match and keep the edges together."

For a moment the machine, which had been borrowed from the inn, hummed a merry song, then teacher looked up to see Dixie sitting very still, her sewing in her lap, while her eyes were gazing between fluttering white curtains and out toward the mountains.

"A penny for your dreams," Miss Bayley called gayly, as she paused to snap a thread.

[185]

Dixie turned, smiling radiantly. "Oh," she laughed, "I was 'magining ahead, I guess. I was wondering what lovely things would happen to Carol in this pretty blue silk dress." Then, a little anxiously, she added, "There'd ought to be a party, shouldn't you think, Miss Bayley?"

"Of course there should be a party, and, what is more, there shall be one, too. When is Carol to have a birthday?"

"November sixth, and that comes on Saturday," the little girl replied. "I was meaning to make a cake, and there'd ought to be one more candle. Grandma Piggins gave Carol eight little candles last year, but now we need nine."

Miss Bayley was again treading the machine and making it hum. Then, when she paused to adjust the ruffler, she glanced up brightly to find that the gold-brown eyes were still watching, apparently waiting. "We'll have that party, dear," the girl-teacher declared, "and the one more candle, I'll promise that, but I'm going to keep it for a surprise for all of you little Martins."

[186]

"Oh, Miss Bayley," said the small girl, clapping her hands gleefully, "won't that be the nicest? It'll be a 'sprise for Baby Jim and for Ken and me, too, as well as for Carol."

Teacher nodded, though at that particular moment she had not the vaguest idea what the surprise-party was to be. Then she added "When is *your* birthday, Dixie, dear?"

"Mine? Oh, I came in February, on the snowiest, coldest, blustriest day, dad said. Brother Ken was born in April, but Baby Jim," the girl's voice softened to a tone of infinite tenderness when she spoke that name, "our little treasure-baby was born on Christmas day." Then she added with that far-away expression which was so often in her eyes, "Grandmother Piggins said when little souls are sent to our earth on Christ's birthday, they have been specially chosen to be His disciples."

[187]

"It may be true, dear." Miss Bayley had thought so little of these things. She had been brought up in boarding-schools without loved ones to guide. Then she added, as she adjusted a long, straight piece of blue silk that was soon to be a ruffle. "Of one thing I am sure, and that is that the influence of a beautiful life lives here on earth long after the form of the loved one has passed from our sight. Grandmother Piggins must have been a dear, dear old lady."

"She was," the child said simply. "Everybody loved her."

"What epitaph could one more desire?" was what the girl-teacher thought. Then the machine began to hum, and Dixie bent over to watch the spindle fly, and to see the strip of silk that was straight on one side come out in the prettiest ruffle on the other.

"I'm glad it's near the end of October now," the small girl said with a little sigh, "for I just couldn't wait more'n two weeks to give that dress to Carol."

[188]

Then, as there was no more basting that she could do, Dixie wandered about the pleasant, home-like room, reading the titles on the books that were everywhere in evidence. Suddenly she paused before a photograph. "Why, Miss Bayley," she exclaimed, "the boy in this picture looks almost 'zactly like you."

"He is my brother, dear, two years younger than I am," the girl-teacher replied, looking up with a smile.

"Oh, I remember now, you did tell me you had a brother Tim. Is he coming West some time to see you, Miss Bayley?"

[189]

There was a sudden shadow on the lovely face that bent over the blue silk. "I'm afraid Tim doesn't care to find me," she said. "I haven't heard from him in over a year. I don't even know where he is. Brother and I were left orphans when I was eight and he six. That was just twelve years ago. Although he is but eighteen, he is a giant of a chap, and would pass for twenty-one. Our guardian put me in a fashionable boarding-school in New York, and placed Tim in a military academy in the South. After that we saw very little of each other, but we did write, that is, I wrote every week and my brother replied now and then, but over a year ago his letters ceased coming, and so, when I graduated and was ready to do what I liked, I went South and visited the academy, only to find that my brother was not there. He had found military discipline too severe, his room-mate told me, and had disappeared. No one knew where he went, but his pal believed that he had gone to sea. Tim had said to him, 'Tell Sis that I'll turn up in three years, if not sooner.' With Tim gone, I had no one in all the world, Dixie, for whom I really cared, and no one cared for me. I was so weary of the noise and artificial life of New York City, and I didn't want to open up our father's home on Riverside Drive without Tim, so I left it all and came West to seek—to seek— Oh, Dixie, dear, I don't know what I came to seek, but I do know what I found." With a little half-sob, the girl-teacher held out both arms, and Dixie went to her.

"I found some one to love, and some one to love me." Then, hastily wiping her eyes, Miss Bayley smilingly declared, "It never would do to get a little salty spot on this lovely blue silk." Then, springing up, she added gayly, "Come now, Miss Midget, you and I are going to have four-o'clock chocolate."

[190]

During the next hour Dixie thought she had never known her beloved teacher to be so light-hearted and merry, but when the small girl had gone down the cañon trail Josephine Bayley went to her screened-in porch bedroom, and, stretching out her arms toward the sky that was such a deep blue over the mountains, she said, "O Thou who holdest the lands and the seas, take care of my brother, Tim." Then, remembering the child's faith in prayer, she added, "And bring him to me soon."

There was peace in the heart of the girl-teacher as she turned back into the little log cabin, for, once again, she had faith in prayer.

"And a little child shall lead them," she thought as she prepared her evening meal.

[191]

CHAPTER TWENTY-FIVE
WHERE THE TRAIL LED

The little lost, almost hidden, trail haunted Josephine Bayley. She thought of it the next morning when she first awoke. It was still hardly daylight when she sprang from bed. "I'm going to climb it to the very top," she thought, "for where others have been, I, too, can go, and maybe I'll be there in time to see the sun rise."

She quickly donned her khaki hiking-clothes, with the short skirt and bloomers; then, taking a stout, knobbed club that Mr. Enterprise Twiggly had given her for a weapon, should she meet a snake or wildcat, away she started, climbing with eager feet, and singing as soon as she was out of hearing, for the very joy of living.

[192]

When a tangle of brush impeded her progress, she thrust the stick ahead and beat the vines and bushes, and then fearlessly pushed through.

"All properly brought-up snakes are hibernating now," she remarked to an overhanging branch that she had to stoop to pass under. "Poor little snakes," she ruminated, "in the hearts of them they probably are as kindly-intentioned as any of us. They love to live in their wild mountain homes, and they would far rather slip away from us than hurt us, but even the truly harmless ones are always battered to death as soon as they are seen, although in gardens they are of great value, if only gardeners knew."

A bird from somewhere sang to her, just, a joyous morning-song. "Which means that the sun is coming up and I have not reached the top of this little lost trail, and, what is more, I'm not likely to until the day is well advanced," said the girl to herself. This because of a dense growth of pine that arose just ahead of her. Then it was that Josephine Bayley noticed that the old trail had evidently been abandoned, for crossing it was a newer one that had been recently used. With a little skip of delight, the girl-teacher turned into the new trail that led through the pine clump, and, ascending easily, to her great joy she saw one of the lower peaks just above her.

[193]

"Oh! oh!" she thought happily. "How I have longed to know what lay beyond this mountain that is in my dooryard, so to speak. I do hope it is not merely another and higher range. Well, I soon shall know."

With feet that seemed tireless, the girl-teacher climbed the short steep bit of trail that was left, and stood at the very summit. Then, with arms outflung, she cried aloud: "Oh, the wonder of it! Now I know how Balboa must have felt when he first beheld the Pacific."

Lake Tahoe, a great sheet of glistening blue, framed in the gray of jagged cliffs and the dark green of encircling pines, lay not many miles beyond. The sun, still near the horizon, was pouring its molten gold over the water, sky, and mountains, transforming them to celestial loveliness. With clasped hands the girl-teacher stood, gazing with her very soul in her eyes. Her hat had been thrown on a rock near by, and the breeze from the lake was tossing her curling locks back from her forehead.

[194]

Little did she dream how beautiful she looked, and still less did she dream that she was being observed by some one who thought her the loveliest creature he had ever seen.

Fifteen minutes passed before the girl became conscious of her surroundings. Not far from the summit, and near a clump of sheltering pines, she saw a camp-fire, and the coals were smoldering. Some one must be near, she thought. For one panicky moment she realized how unprotected, how very much alone, she was on that high peak, but, as no one appeared, she decided that the camper had gone his way, and she, too, turned, and, after one more glance back at the water, retraced her steps to her cabin home.

But the camper had not gone. He had been lying very still behind a great gray boulder. He knew that this maiden had climbed the trail, wishing to be alone, and, too, he had reasons of his own for not desiring to make his presence known.

As Josephine Bayley descended the trail, her fancy followed the mysterious camper, wondering what he might look like,—a hoary-bearded prospector, perhaps, still hunting for that elusive vein of silver. Had she seen the young man who stood erect soon after her departure, had she noted his square chin, his gray, far-seeing eyes, his keen, kind face, tanned by the beating of sun and wind, sleet and rain, she would have been more interested and curious than ever.

CHAPTER TWENTY-SIX
KEN'S QUEST

When the pupils gathered on Monday morning, Miss Bayley soon realized that the little Martins had something to tell her that they believed was of great interest. It was indeed astonishing and most acceptable news. Carol, who had spent Saturday afternoon on the Valley Ranch, had been informed by Sue Piggins that little Jessica Archer was to return with her to the boarding-school in Reno. Mrs. Sethibald, the mother, had let it be known that a common log-cabin school was not good enough for a "sheep-princess," and that from then on she was to have the best "iddication" that could be obtained, for, like as not, when she was grown, she'd be one of the first ladies of Nevada, if not of the whole land.

"The girls over there won't like her, not the least little mite," Sue had prophesied, "that is, not unless she changes a lot. Their fathers are all more educated, and just as rich as Mr. Archer is or ever will be."

Miss Bayley said little when this news was told, but secretly she rejoiced. She had feared that she would be obliged by the law to report Jessica as a truant if she did not attend school anywhere, but it surely was not pleasant to anticipate her return to the little log school in Woodford's Cañon.

So happy, indeed, did the girl-teacher feel that she wished that it were within her power to declare a half-holiday, but, since it was not, she decided to close half an hour early and take all her little pupils, Mexicans, blacksmith's son, and the trapper's two little girls, who always looked hungry, with the four Martins, over to her cabin to celebrate. Even while she was giving out sums in mathematics her thoughts were straying. "I'm so glad I made a mountain of a chocolate cake," she was thinking; "and I'll make more chocolate to drink, and for once Milly and Maggy Mullett, at least, shall have all the cake they wish."

[198]

Mrs. Sethibald Archer would indeed have been indignant if she had known her daughter's withdrawal from the log-cabin school was being considered an occasion for especial rejoicing.

Often during the morning Dixie glanced at Miss Bayley and thought that she never before had noticed how very young-looking she was, and, too, the girl-teacher looked as though she might begin to sing at any minute. Indeed, so real was Miss Bayley's desire to do so that she quite upset the usual plan of study by saying: "Don't let's do mathematics any more this morning. Let's each choose a song to sing." Which they did, and how the little old schoolhouse rang, for each chose a song that they all knew well, and although little Dixie, who led them, had not the vaguest idea why teacher was so happy, the spirit of rejoicing was contagious, and her birdlike soprano voice trilled sweeter and higher, encouraging those who faltered.

[199]

When at last the solemn-faced clock, which perhaps had been watching all this unusual procedure with dignified surprise, slowly tolled the hour of ten, Miss Bayley said: "And now we will have recess. Dixie, dear, will you lead the games to-day, and Ken, will you remain with me? I wish to speak to you."

The heart of loyal little Ken was filled with pride. It was a great honor, the pupils of Josephine Bayley thought, to be asked to remain in at recess and be talked to by teacher. Sometimes she actually asked their opinions about things, for, strange as it may seem, it was her theory that if the children would rather have red geraniums blossoming on the window-sill, instead of white, red they should be.

"It's *your* schoolroom," she had told her pupils, "and here you spend the heart of every day. I want it to be beautiful in your eyes, and then I know it will be in mine."

Was there ever another teacher so understanding as their beloved Miss Bayley?

Ken's intelligent freckled face glowed with eagerness when at last the little line of pupils had filed out to the playground, and he was to hear why Miss Bayley had asked him to stay in at recess.

[200]

The young teacher left her desk and stepped down by his side. "Laddie," she began, "yesterday morning early I climbed the trail that starts back of the inn, and I found a wonderful view of Lake Tahoe, but I found more than that. Guess what?"

She had placed a hand on each of his shoulders, and was looking into the wondering eyes that were so like Dixie's, though not so dreamy, for Ken was a doer of deeds, as Pine Tree Martin had been.

"Oh, Miss Bayley, teacher, what? A bear, like 'twas. Now and then they do come down from the high Nevadas, but usually not till the snows set in."

"Gracious, me, no, not that. If I had met a bear, I don't suppose I should be here to-day to tell about it."

The girl-teacher looked her consternation at the mere possibility of such a meeting, but the boy shook his head, with its unruly mop of hair that was redder than Dixie's, as he answered, "Bears don't touch people unless they're cornered or come upon sudden-like."

[201]

Then, remembering that the mystery had not been explained, he asked eagerly, "Miss Bayley, what *did* you see?"

"A camp-fire, Ken, and although no one at all was in sight, the coals were still smoldering. Now, who do you suppose would be breakfasting on that high peak? It isn't a trail that leads anywhere in particular, is it?"

"The Washoe Indians go over that way to Lake Tahoe fishing, but it doesn't sound like Indians," the boy said. Then his eyes lighted with hope. "Do you 'spose maybe 'twas a train-robber hiding?"

"Goodness, I hope not!" Miss Bayley shuddered. "I'd heaps rather have met your bear." Then she added, "Have there been any trains robbed lately?"

The boy had to confess that he hadn't heard of any. "There used to be lots of train and stage hold-ups when my dad was a boy," he said, "but nowdays nothing much happens." There was real regret in the tone of the lad, as though life in the Sierra Nevadas had become too tame to be of real interest. Then his eyes again brightened. "Well, anyhow, it might have been a sheep-rustler. How I'd like to trail him, if 'twas. There's a State bounty for cornering one, Miss Bayley."

[202]

The girl-teacher laughed at the boy's eagerness. "Well, Ken," she confessed, "all I saw was a smoldering camp-fire, and since a bear, a coyote, or a mountain lion cannot make a fire, we shall have to believe that a man had breakfasted there at sunrise, but I heard no one and saw no one."

"Oh, Miss Bayley, teacher, how I'd like to 'vestigate. I'd like to, *awful well*, if I could get 'scused a little early. It gets dusky so soon now, and I'd need to have two hours of daylight, certain."

This was an unusual and unexpected request, but the holiday spirit was in the heart of the girl-teacher, and so, to the great joy of the lad, she granted it. Then she added, as a new thought suggested itself: "I don't know, dear boy, that I *ought* to let you go, if you think it *might* be a bandit in hiding, or anything like that. Would you be safe?"

[203]

The boy's expression was hard for Miss Bayley to interpret. "Oh, teacher! Boys aren't scared of bandits. They like 'em! You know that Robin Hood fellow in the book you and Dixie bought me in Reno. Now, he was a bandit, wasn't he? A reg'lar bandit."

The girl-teacher had to agree. "But, Ken," she protested feebly, "he was a story-book bandit. They are different in real life, aren't they?"

"I dunno," the boy had to acknowledge. "I haven't met one yet, but I'd like to. Gee whiz, Miss Bayley, I wish I could start right now. I sure do! Maybe he's goin' on somewhere else this afternoon. Maybe I'd catch him if I went this very minute."

Miss Bayley laughed. She knew that it was her fault, for she had filled the boy's mind with longing for adventure, and she also knew that he would be unable to study that day, and so she said, "But you haven't had your lunch."

"I've got my share in my pocket this minute. Could I go, Miss Bayley? Could I go now?"

[204]

What was there to do but agree, and, with a little half-suppressed whoop of joy, the boy leaped to the row of hats, snatched his own from a hook, waved it in farewell, and was gone. A wild gazelle could hardly have been more fleet of foot.

No stick did he carry to beat ahead for snakes. This little lad, born and reared in the mountains, had no fear of the other creatures dwelling there. With understanding sympathy and comradeship he made them all his friends.

[205]

CHAPTER TWENTY-SEVEN
CELEBRATING

The holiday spirit continued to pervade the little log schoolhouse, and Dixie marveled, for was not this Monday, the day of the week when lessons were usually the hardest? Then, at two o'clock, and right in the middle of the spelling recitation, Miss Bayley closed the book, and, placing it in her desk, made an unprecedented announcement, "Suppose we speak pieces for a while, and then I have a surprise planned for you."

Unable longer to keep from expressing her curiosity, the slim, freckled hand of Dixie went up. The beaming teacher nodded, and the little maid rose and inquired, "Miss Bayley, is it your birthday to-day?"

[206]

The girl-teacher laughed aloud. "I feel as though it were," she confessed. "I am almost sure it is, somehow. We might call it an extra make-believe birthday, for my real one comes in January when it's blustery and cold."

Then, following up the idea suggested by the pupil she so loved, she asked, "How many of you would like to come to my extra-birthday party?"

How the hands flew up! The suggestion of it was beyond the understanding of some of them, but "party" was a word known to all except the little Mexicans. However, even their small brown hands went up, and their smiles were as bright as the smiles of those who fully comprehended the meaning of the magical word.

"Very well, but first we will have an hour of reading and recitation. Now, Jimmy-Boy, will you begin by speaking one of your seven pieces?"

The curly-headed little fellow who sat at the big double desk with Dixie, dangling feet that were too short to reach the floor, slipped down and went very willingly up to the platform, where he made his little bow and began to recite, but instead of speaking one of his seven pieces, he kept right on saying them all, for they were but Mother Goose rhymes, and none of them long.

[207]

He was so irresistibly cunning that every one clapped, even Mercedes and Franciscito. Miss Bayley, noting their dark, beaming faces, choosing words that she had taught them, asked if they could not do something.

To her surprise, the little black-eyed girl arose and replied in her soft, musical voice, "*Si, senorita.*" Then, taking her brother by the hand, she led him to the rostrum, and together they sang a Spanish serenade, and so beautifully that Miss Bayley and Dixie were indeed delighted.

Then the solemn-faced grandfather's clock, which perhaps was still shocked at such unusual levity on a workaday Monday in the schoolroom over which it presided, very slowly announced that the hour was three.

"Good!" Miss Bayley cried, seeming very like a girl herself in the mood of the day. "Now we'll have that extra-birthday party."

[208]

Out of the little log schoolhouse they trooped, half an hour early, that none might be later than usual reaching their homes. Over to "dear teacher's" they went, and were served with very large slices of that wonderful mountain chocolate cake, with more chocolate to drink. Then, with a loving pat for each little one, Miss Bayley dismissed them, holding fast all the time to the hand of the pupil she loved the best. When the others had gone on ahead, Josephine Bayley stooped, and kissing Dixie on the forehead, she said softly, "Come over early next Saturday afternoon, dear, and we will finish the blue-silk dress."

When she was alone the girl-teacher wondered if her joyous mood was altogether because of the departure of the troublesome pupil. Was it not rather a premonition of some new and wonderful interest that was to come into her life? If troubles cast their shadows ahead, even more does joy illumine the way it treads.

CHAPTER TWENTY-EIGHT
ON THE TRAIL OF A "BANDIT"

Up through the old trail the boy had broken his way, and into the newer, more open path he leaped, his feet winged with eagerness, and it was a very breathless lad who at last reached the trail's end and found the cold gray ashes that had been a camp-fire.

"He's gone!" he said aloud. "Whoever 'twas has gone on farther." Then, as he glanced among the near pines, he thought, "I might have known he'd be gone by this time. A sheep-rustler, or a bandit, either, wouldn't just stay on a mountain-peak."

Truly disappointed, the boy climbed to the highest point, and, shading his eyes, looked in every direction.

The sun was high, the lake a deep emerald hue, with here and there the reflection of a fleecy white cloud slowly drifting across its mirror-like surface, for not a breath of air was stirring. Then the lad's gaze swept the mountain-ranges beyond.

"Guess I'm not much good at catching sheep-rustlers," he commented, "but then, I wouldn't think much of one, or a bandit either, who'd sit here and wait to be caught."

The lad suddenly realized that he was very hungry. He sat on a rock near, and looked meditatively about as he munched on the sandwich which he had taken from his pocket.

Suddenly he leaped to his feet, ran a little way toward the burned-out camp-fire, and, kneeling, examined the ground. A footprint! It hadn't been made by the soft leather shoe that Washoe Indians often wore. Rising, and still munching his bread and meat, he placed his own smaller foot in the print.

"Whoever he is, he's a big fellow!" he said admiringly. "A reg'lar giant." Then, having finished the bread, he drew a rosy apple from the depth of another pocket where it had been bulging. The boy walked about, poking in the ashes; then suddenly, with a whoop of delight, he knelt down, jammed the remaining piece of apple in his mouth to dispose of it speedily, and with his freed hands drew forth a sheet of partly burned, much-blackened paper that had writing on it.

"Whizzle!" he ejaculated. "How I hope it's a clue."

He spread the paper on a flat boulder, and knelt to examine it closely. The fire and the smoke had done their best to make it hard for him to decipher the finely written words. It seemed to be the fragment of a personal letter written to a relative, but not one reference was made to holding up a train or rustling sheep. At the very bottom, in a scorched place, the boy found something which caused him to leap to his feet and prance about as a wild Indian would, when celebrating a joyous occasion.

"Hurray! Hurray!" he fairly shouted, and the near peak echoed back the cry. Then, climbing again to the highest boulder, the lad once more shaded his eyes, this time with an even greater eagerness to discover some sign of a camp. At last, over on the next mountain which was so perilously steep that few attempted to scale it, and up near the top, the boy's eyes found what he sought—a camp-fire.

"Ginger!" he thought. "I don't know how he ever got there, whoever he is. Climbing that mountain is like trying to shin up the wall of a barn, but if he can do it, so can I, but 'twould take me a day, and it's too late now."

The boy looked toward the west, and saw the sun was low in the horizon. "I'd go to-morrow, but Dixie wouldn't like it if I cut school, and I'd ought to stick at arithmetic if I'm going to be a civil engineer. But I'll come up here Saturday before sun-up, and if that camp's over there then, I'm going to head for it, and if it's who I think maybe 'tis— Aw—but, gee, it couldn't be. Well, it's somebody, and who it is I want to find out."

"There wasn't anybody there," was the report he gave Miss Bayley the next day. "Whoever it was made the fire had moved on." He said nothing of his plans, but it was very hard for the boy, yearning for adventure, to keep his mind on mathematics that week, and Saturday was a long time coming.

But come it did, and hours before the sun was up Ken was on the trail, eager, expectant.

Again on the top of the trail where the burnt-out camp-fire had been discovered, Ken scrambled to the peak of the highest boulder, and, with a heart beating like a trip-hammer, he pulled his wide-brimmed hat over his eyes to shade them from the glare of the sun that was rising in a cloudless sky.

Would there be any sign of the camp on the mountains beyond, he wondered. Even as he looked he decided that whether there was or not, he would not return to Woodford's without having further investigated.

At first the lad saw nothing but the dazzling golden light of the sun that was slowly rising higher, driving the gloom from the cañons, but, as he continued to gaze, faint and far he saw a thin column of smoke wavering uncertainly, and then suddenly drop down, to rise again a moment later, as though invigorated when fresh and more inflammable fuel had been added to the fire.

The lad scrambled down from his peak of observation and danced about as he shouted aloud, to the very evident astonishment of a squirrel near by: "He's there! That is, somebody's there, and, oh, if it should be— But I mustn't get my heart set on that."

Then he looked again to make sure that he had not been imagining. It might be mist or haze, but there it was, unmistakably rising in a straight, unwavering dark line against the gleaming blue of the sky. Then, as the boy watched, a breeze, wafting across the lake, waved the column of smoke.

"I feel sort o' like an Indian trying to read smoke-signals," he thought gleefully; "only, whoever made that fire isn't trying to send messages to me. If it's a bandit hiding there, he wouldn't want any one to know where he is even. Gee, he might be a dangerous character! Maybe I'd better steal up soft-like so that I can make a good getaway without his knowin' I'm about, if—"

[215]

Then he chuckled as he started down the trail on the other side of the low peak. "Dixie's the one in our family who is supposed to have 'magination," he thought; "but this morning my head seems to be full of queer notions."

At first he started to sing, a glad shouting kind of song without words or meaning except that he was eager, excited, and happy. But suddenly he stopped as though fearing that some wanton wind would carry his voice to the lone man who was probably then breakfasting.

Ken was following the trail that had been made by the Washoe Indians from the cañon, when they went over to Lake Tahoe to fish, but at last the boy left it and broke through the sagebrush and other tangled growths and began climbing a trailless way toward the highest mountain near Woodford's, which rose bare, gray, grim, lonely, forbidding.

There were times in the ascent when Ken came to a sheer wall, higher than his head, and, to scale it, he took off his shoes, knotted the strings, flung them over his shoulder, and then went up, clinging to crevices with his toes and finger-tips.

[216]

It was lucky that Dixie, the little mother of them all, could not see just then, the brother she so loved, for he was often in most perilous positions, where a single slip would have sent him hurtling on the jagged rocks far below. But his desire to reach the goal of his dreams gave him strength and skill, it would seem, and soon he reached the first small plateau and there he sat, the sun at its zenith assuring him that it was noon. Taking the inevitable sandwich from his pocket, he ate it hungrily. Then he stretched out on the flat rock, conscious of strained muscles and glad of a moment's rest. But it wasn't long before he had leaped to his feet and rejoiced to find that, around the outjutting rocks, there was a belt of scraggly low-growing pines. To these he could cling and make greater progress. How near was he to the camp, he wondered. Suddenly he paused and listened intently.

[217]

A gunshot rang out so close to the boy that instinctively he dropped to the ground, pressing close behind a boulder. What could it mean? Was he nearer the camp than he had supposed? Had the bandit, or whoever was in hiding, seen him or heard him? This was possible, as but a moment before he had slipped, displacing some loose stones that had rattled noisily down the mountain-side.

Or, if he had caused a motion among the dwarf pines to which he was clinging, as he made the ascent, he might have been taken for a skulking coyote or a mountain-lion.

Almost breathlessly the lad waited, listening, watching, but he heard nothing and no one came. Fifteen minutes passed before he dared to go on, and even then he did not stand erect, but crouched, keeping hidden by the stunted growths about him.

This was the big adventure that his boyish heart had yearned for, and the real element of danger but enhanced his joy in it.

He was wondering how much farther he would have to go before he saw signs of a camp, when suddenly he rounded a denser and higher clump of trees and found himself looking directly into a clearing on a small plateau, which was protected on three sides, the fourth opening toward the lake. Darting back under cover of the low-growing pines, Ken peered out and beheld a rude structure that was neither cabin nor wigwam, but a shelter made of green branches. The campfire in front of it was still smoldering, proving that either the man was not far away, or that he had not long been gone. Then a terrible fear smote the heart of the lad. What if that had been the camper's last meal on the mountain! What if he had now departed, not to return!

Just at that moment another shot rang out, the sound reverberating from the cañon below. The camper was evidently hunting for game. Indeed he probably had nothing else to eat, though lower down and near the lake there were rushing streams in which the little mountain trout could be caught in abundance.

The lad hardly knew what to do. He feared it would not be wise for him to go boldly into this unknown man's camp while he was away, for if it should be one of the "dangerous characters" occasionally described by the Genoa "Crier," who sought a hiding-place in the high Nevadas, the lad would want to slip away unobserved.

He decided to remain under cover until the camper had returned. Luckily, Ken had not long to wait, for a nearer shot told that the hunter was approaching, and in another moment a tall, sinewy, broad-shouldered young man swung into view, a small deer flung over his shoulder.

His brown hair was long and his face nearly covered with a beard. Indeed, at first glance, he looked as though he might be a very dangerous character, but just as Ken had made this decision, the young man, little knowing that he was being so closely observed, began to sing in a tenor voice that carried to the heart of the listener the conviction that, whatever might be the reason for his hiding, it was not because of an evil record.

However, he did not leave his place of observation at once. He watched as the young giant dropped the small deer upon the ground, stretched his arms out as though to rest them, and then disappeared in his pine shelter. A moment later he reappeared without the gun, and carrying a long sharp knife. Kneeling by the deer, he prepared to skin it.

Silently the lad drew nearer, but so intent was the camper upon his occupation that he did not hear a footfall nor a sound of any kind until the boy spoke hesitatingly, "I say, mister, I'm awful good at skinning creatures. Couldn't I help?"

The young man, who had believed himself to be alone near the top of an almost unscaleable mountain, leaped to his feet, amazed. His keen gray eyes swept over the very small figure of the barefooted boy, and then, to the unutterable joy of the lad, his hands were seized and a voice he knew and loved was fairly shouting: "Ken Martin, old pal; I've been wondering how in time I could get word to you that I was—well, sort of a neighbor of yours. I fully intended to drop down into Woodford's soon and hunt you up, but I'm mighty glad you called first, so to speak. Sit down, old man. But wait; I'll get you a drink of aqua pura from my near-by sparkling fount. You look petered out, as though you had climbed to near the end of your strength."

[221]

The boy drank long of the water which was given him in a folding cup, and then, as he sank down on the ground in a truly weary heap, he gasped, "I say, Mr. Edrington, what-all are you doing up here?"

[222]

CHAPTER TWENTY-NINE
KEN'S OLD FRIEND

"Ken, you've been doing some growing since we put the highway through your cañon two years ago." The young man, with folded arms, stood smiling down at the boy, who grinned back as he replied with enthusiasm, "If I can keep right on till I'm big as you are, I'll like it mighty well."

"I believe you'll make it," Frederick Edrington declared as he seated himself upon a boulder near and continued to look approvingly at the lad. "You remember what I used to tell you about getting what you want?"

[223]

The boy nodded his red-brown mop of hair. "Yeah," he said, lapsing unconsciously into the speech of the mountaineers. "First fix a definite goal, it doesn't matter how far ahead or how rough the road in between, and then keep going toward it."

"Even if you slip back two steps for every one that you forge ahead," his companion put in.

Ken laughed. "Gee, I hope it won't be as hard as all that for me to get to be a civil engineer."

The eyes of the older man lighted. "Still holding that for a goal, boy?" he asked, his voice showing his real pleasure.

Ken nodded. "Bet I am," he replied.

"Worked hard at math?" was the next query. "Pretty quick at doing sums?"

Ken flushed. "I don't know as I'm a crackerjack at it, but I told Miss Bayley all about how I want to grow up to be just like you, and when she found I wanted to get along faster in arithmetic, she stayed after school to help me whenever the sums were extra hard. I say, Mr. Edrington, our new teacher, she's a trump!"

The young civil engineer, who had been leaning back, hands locked behind his head, sat up with sudden interest.

"Kind of a thin, skinny, old-maid sort of a person, is she?" he asked with a smile lurking away back in his gray eyes.

"Indeed she is not!" Ken retorted loyally. "Miss Bayley, next to my mother, is the most beautiful woman that ever lived at Woodford's or anywhere in all the world I guess. Even queens couldn't be nicer, and she isn't thin or homely, though I guess she is pretty old." Then he dug his bare toes in the dry pine-needles as he added, looking at his friend speculatively, "I guess she's nearly as old as you are."

Mr. Edrington's amused laughter rang out. "Poor girl, if she's that ancient, she'd better be saving her pennies, for she'll soon be ready for the Old Ladies' Home."

Ken, solemn-eyed, watched the speaker. "She isn't that old," he said. "I know, for there's an old folks' home over toward Genoa, but the people are bent and sort of hobble and lean on sticks when they walk. I guess, come to think of it, maybe Miss Bayley isn't what you'd call real old yet." Then his face lighted with admiration. "Gee, but she's a good sport, though! She held the pig for me the first day she came to our house while I made the pen, and she didn't squeal at all."

"Lucky pig!" the young man commented.

This went over the head of the boy, who remarked laughingly, "The pig didn't think so. He wriggled so hard, trying to get away, and you just should have heard him squeal. But, gee, didn't that prove teacher is a brick? Most girls, except Dixie, would have said they wouldn't even touch a little pig. They aren't much good, girls aren't, except Dixie and—well, Carol, she's doin' better."

Mr. Edrington steered the conversation into channels in which he was interested.

"Any newcomers down at the inn?" he inquired, looking closely at the lad. The boy shook his head. "Don't think so," he said, "none that I've heard of. Why?"

"Well, I was hoping that there were none," was the non-committal reply. Then he added, "Open an ear, old pal, for if you swear to secrecy, I'm going to tell you why I'm here."

"Cross my heart and hope to die if I ever do tell," the boy promised so solemnly that the young man wanted to smile, but thought best to accept the oath as seriously as it had been made.

"Well, it sounds foolish, I know, but I'm hiding from an aunt of mine who wants me to marry an heiress, and since the girl herself agrees with my aunt, I knew my only safety lay in flight. Everywhere I went I was pursued by this elderly relative, who, having brought me up since my parents died, thinks that she owns me body and soul. I do feel a sincere depth of gratitude toward her, but prefer to pay it in some other way than by marrying the girl of her choice, an alliance with whom, I have been assured every day for the past year, would greatly add to my fame and fortune."

As he paused the boy looked up sympathetically. "Gee, I don't wonder you hid," he commented. "You wouldn't catch me getting married. I'd heaps rather go to sea, maybe to China, or do something exciting."

"H-m! A very sensible decision, my lad, and yet the sea of matrimony, I've been told, is not without its exciting adventures." Then the civil engineer laughed. "Romance is a little beyond your comprehension, and I'm glad it is. It will be a relief to hear about something else for a time. I'm not in love, never was in love, and don't believe I ever shall be in love."

Why was it, at that very moment, and quite without will of his own, Frederick Edrington saw in his memory a slim young girl standing silhouetted against a gleaming morning sky, with arms outflung and curling brown hair blown about a face so lovely that it had haunted him every hour, waking or sleeping, that had passed since he had first beheld the vision?

"I say, Ken," he suddenly remarked, "that new teacher of yours, has she soft curly, brown hair, and does she wear a khaki hiking-suit—short skirt and bloomers?"

The boy nodded, then exclaimed as he suddenly recalled something: "Gee whiz! Mr. Edrington, I clean forgot it was teacher who started me out on this hunt for you. 'Course she didn't know it was you, but the other morning, when she climbed to the top of the Little Peak trail to see the sun rise, she saw a camp-fire, and she asked me if I could guess who might have made it. I sort of hoped it was a sheep-rustler, and Miss Bayley—gee, but she's a sport, all right—let me out of school early that day so I could go up and see who was there, and then it was I saw smoke over here, and thought I'd climb up and see who it might be. I found a piece of a letter in the ashes that day, and one word was 'engineering.' It made me hope,—how I did hope,—maybe it was you," then, triumphantly, "and it was."

"Rather is, son," was the reply. Then the young man rose as he remarked. "Wish you could stay till the snow falls."

The boy's eyes opened wide. "Mr. Edrington," he exclaimed, "you aren't going to stay up here all winter, are you? Why, you'll be frozen stiff."

The young man laughed as he knelt to skin the small deer. But he spoke with decision. "I shall stay in this impenetrable fastness until I hear that the lovely Marlita Arden has married a certain Lord Dunsbury, who really wants her, or wants her millions, I don't know which, nor do I care. Marlita thinks that she loves me, but nevertheless she will soon decide that it is better to have a titled spouse than a humble engineer, and until she does reach that decision the name of Frederick Edrington will be found among those reported missing; missing, anyway, from fashionable Washington society, where he has had to be more or less active for the past two years."

"Well," Ken said rather wistfully, "if you're going to stay, I kind o' wish I could stay, too, but I don't know how Dixie could get on without me to bring the wood and make the fires, and—" The boy's face suddenly brightened, and, leaping up, he did his wild Indian dance. Then, landing in front of the astonished onlooker, he concluded with a whoop: "I say, Mr. Edrington, if you want to hide, I know where's the best place, and you could be right with me, with us, I mean."

"Where?" the young man was curious.

[230]

"In our loft bedroom. Dixie and Carol'd just as soon sleep down-stairs, and you could sleep up there and have a rope-ladder that you could draw up, and no aunts could ever find you. Then, between stages, you'd be safe enough and could go where you'd like. Oh, I say, Mr. Edrington, will you come?"

The young man held out his big hand and grasped the smaller freckled one. "Maybe later I'll take you up on that," he said, "but at present I'm using this location as a problem in mining engineering—just for practice-work, old man." Then he smiled speculatively. "But I'll promise this: If the lovely Marlita has not wed this Lord Dunsbury by the time the first snow comes, I'll drop down to Woodford's, and take up my abode in your loft room, and thanks, old pal, for wanting me."

Then, as it was mid-afternoon, the boy thought he'd better be starting back, and the engineer pointed out a much easier way of descent, which he had discovered. "I'll come next Saturday again, Mr. Edrington. Is there anything I can pack up for you?"

[231]

"Yes, son. Bring me a Reno paper if you can get hold of one, and a book to read, history preferred; and, by the way, kid, remember your hope-to-die promise. You might tell your teacher that a hairy old hermit named Rattlesnake Sam lives on the mountain, and that he it was who built the fire that she saw."

The boy grinned his appreciation. "All right," he said, "I'm game." Then he started away, looking back with a longing to stay, but his loyal little heart knew that Dixie would have need of his services, and so he hurried down the trail and reached Woodford's in half the time it had taken to make the ascent.

[232]

CHAPTER THIRTY
"RATTLESNAKE SAM"

"Teacher, Miss Bayley." The boy who spoke was standing on the doorstep of the small cabin near the inn.

"Why, Ken, good-morning. You are up very early, aren't you," the young woman who had opened the door exclaimed in surprise. Then, with sudden anxiety, "Is anything wrong at your home? Are Dixie, Carol, and the baby all right?"

The boy's freckled face was beaming, and about his manner there was something suggestive of suppressed excitement. "Oh, yes'm, thank you, teacher. 'Tisn't about the girls I have come." Then, almost with embarrassment, he twisted one bare foot over the other and looked down. He had sworn an oath to Frederick Edrington that he wouldn't tell any one who the camper on the peak had been, and it was hard, very hard for the son of Pine Tree Martin to tell anything but the square and honest truth.

[233]

Miss Bayley, watching the boy, was indeed puzzled. "Dear," she said kindly, placing a hand on his shoulder, "come in, won't you? I'm sure you haven't had breakfast yet. Please stay and share mine with me."

The boy's red-brown eyes lifted quickly. "Oh, no'm, teacher, thanks; I couldn't do that. I told Dixie I'd be back, and she'll be waiting, but I—I wanted to tell you that I found the—the man who had made the campfire that you saw."

Miss Bayley was interested at once. "Oh, Ken," she said, drawing the lad within and closing the door. "Surely you can spare a minute to tell me about him. Was he a sheep-rustler or a train-robber or a bandit, or whatever it was you hoped he would be?"

The boy shook his mop of red-brown hair and looked away to hide the joy that was in his eyes when he remembered who it had been that he had found. "No'm, Miss Bayley! He said that he was a hermit, and that his name was—er—Rattlesnake Sam."

[234]

"Oh, how interesting, Ken," the girl-teacher exclaimed. "I've always loved to read stories about the West; perhaps that was why I was so eager to come when I was free to do as I pleased; and one of the things that fascinated me was the way the men changed their names. I often wondered what had happened in their lives to cause their comrades to call them the strange things they did. Of course Dick Sureshot, Broncho Bill, and names like that are easy to understand, and 'Rattlesnake Sam' merely means, I suppose, that this old hermit has killed a great many rattlers. He is a very, very old man, isn't he?"

"Yes'm, Miss Bayley. That is, no'm, I mean. I guess he isn't a hundred yet."

The girl-teacher laughed. "Ken," she said, "it's plain to see that you were terribly disappointed to find merely a hermit when you had hoped to trail a sheep-rustler. Confess now, you are disappointed, aren't you?"

[235]

Miss Bayley insisted that the boy look at her, and when he did, she found herself puzzled at the glow that his eager eyes held. But, before she could question him further, the lad was saying, "Miss Bayley, teacher, the old hermit said he wished he had something to read, and that's why I came over this morning. After school this afternoon he's coming halfway down the trail, and I'm going half-way up, and I said I'd ask you to loan me a book for him."

"Oho, so your old hermit can read! Well, I'm glad to hear that." Then the girl-teacher turned toward the book-shelves as she said meditatively, "I wonder what kind of books old hermits like best. One about snakes, do you suppose? I sent for one after Mrs. Enterprise Twiggly told me that it was hard for a tenderfoot to tell a stick from a snake just at first. Now, whenever I go out, I take along the book, but as yet I haven't met a snake."

"No'm, you're not likely to," Ken said; "not till spring comes again."

[236]

While he spoke the boy's eyes roved about, and suddenly he saw a large volume lying on the window-seat. In it was a mark, for indeed, it was the book Josephine Bayley had been reading but the evening before.

Seizing it, he read the title, then lifted an eager face. "Oh, teacher, this one will be just right if you can spare it."

The tone of the young woman expressed her mingled surprise and doubt. "Why, no, Ken, an old hermit would not care for Wells."

But the boy persisted, "Yes'm, teacher, he would. Rattlesnake Sam said he liked history best."

"Very well, dear," Miss Bayley replied meekly. Then she added, "Suppose you take along this new current-events magazine that just came yesterday. Perhaps your old hermit would like that, too."

"Oh, thank you, teacher, Miss Bayley!" How the red-brown eyes were glowing! "An' I'll tell him that you sent 'em, and he'll be just ever so careful of them."

[237]

"I'm sure that he will. Good-by, my boy." Then for a moment the girl stood in the open doorway, watching the bare brown legs that fairly flew down the trail. Turning back to complete the preparation of her breakfast, she found herself trying to picture what the old hermit looked like. "Perhaps he is some dry-as-dust professor, who is studying fossils and rocks. He probably had a long gray beard, a leathery, wrinkled face, and kindly blue eyes that are near-sighted." Then she sighed. Perhaps even Miss Bayley was a little disappointed that the builder of the campfire that had so interested her had proved to be so old and fogyish. "Well, what does it matter? I probably shall never see him," she thought.

CHAPTER THIRTY-ONE
AN UNWELCOME GUEST

As Ken descended the trail leading to his log-cabin home, he was surprised to see a horse and buggy just leaving the drive. In it was no other than the banker from Genoa, who was so loved by the Martin children. He did not seem to see the boy, who hurried on down the trail, his heart filled with dread lest the keeper of their income had been there to report that once again it had diminished.

This fear was confirmed, or so he believed, when he saw Dixie run out of the house and toward him, an expression on her face which plainly told her brother that her heart was perplexed or dismayed.

"Dix, what's the matter? Is the money all gone? I say, Sis, if it's that, don't take it hard. I can go to work driving sheep over to the Valley Ranch any day! Mr. Piggins said so last week."

"'Tisn't money," the girl replied, smiling almost tremulously, "It's something different." Then she glanced toward the open door of the cabin and drew her brother farther away, but he paused and looked back. "Is that Carol crying in there? Why don't you tell me what's happened? I can't understand at all."

As soon as they were out of hearing, the small girl told the story of recent events. "Just after you had gone up to see teacher," she began, "I was cooking the porridge when Carol called that Mr. Clayburn was driving in, and that that horrid Sylvia was with him. Carol hadn't finished dressing yet, and so she was up in the loft, looking out the little window.

"I ran to the door, and, sure enough, that was who it was. Mr. Clayburn seemed to be terribly worried about something, and that peaked little girl of his looked as though she'd 'most cried her eyes out.

"When the buggy stopped, he left little Sylvia on the seat, and he came in and said: 'Dixie Martin, I've come to ask you to do me a great favor. I'm in deep trouble, and no one at this hour can help me as much as you can.' Of course I said, 'Mr. Clayburn, I'll do just anything I can'; and he said, 'I knew you would, Dixie.' Then he told me that his wife had been taken suddenly and very seriously ill, and that she was in a Reno hospital, and that he would have to stay there for a time to be near her, and that he wanted to leave Sylvia with us. Oh, Ken, I just had to say that of course we would take her, even though I knew how Carol feels about her, and so that's what happened. It's Sylvia in there crying, and Carol's up in the loft. I climbed up to tell her 'bout everything, and she said I needn't expect her to come down-stairs as long as that horrid snippy Sylvia Clayburn is in the house. She declared she'd stay up there and starve unless I'd take her breakfast up to her. Oh, Ken, what shall we do? You can't blame Carol, 'cause you know Sylvia was mean and horrid when our little sister was in her home."

The older brother was indeed puzzled.

[241]

He did not blame Carol, for she had been most unkindly treated by the mother and daughter. "I guess we'll have to just do what we can, Dix," he said. "Mr. Clayburn's one of the best friends we've got, and for his sake we'll have to put up with that—that little minx of his."

Dixie had been looking thoughtfully down into the sunlit valley. She could see a group of white buildings partly hidden by cottonwood trees. In her gold-brown eyes was the far-away expression which often suggested to Miss Bayley that the soul of the girl was beholding a vision. The boy's gaze followed hers. Then he turned toward his sister as he said gently: "I know what you're doing. You're trying to remember if Grandmother Piggins ever said anything that would help us. Aren't you, Dix?"

[242]

The girl nodded; then, her eyes alight, she suddenly exclaimed as she caught his free hand,— the other still held the history: "Ken Martin, I have it! I just knew I'd remember something. Once when Sue came home from boarding-school she said that she just hated her room-mate. She was going to be as mean as she could, hoping that the new pupil would ask to have her room changed. But Grandma Piggins said: 'Sue, just to please me, will you try my way for one week? If it doesn't work, then you may try your own.' Of course Sue would do anything to please her dear old grandmother. Then she asked what she was to do.

"Grandma Piggins said: 'It's a game of make-believe. First, pretend, in your own heart, that you like the new pupil, and that you are glad she is your room-mate, and then treat her just as you would if you thought she was the nicest girl you knew, and, by the end of the week, you may find that the pretend has come true.'"

"How did it turn out?" the boy inquired.

"They're still room-mates," Dixie told him. Then she added: "But come on, Ken, we'd better go in. Nobody's had any breakfast, and it's almost school-time." The little mother sighed. "I don't see how I can go to school this morning," she said. "I can't leave Carol up in the loft and Sylvia down-stairs crying her heart out, and neither of them speaking to each other."

[243]

"I'll go to school and take Baby Jim and tell teacher that maybe you three girls will be along in the afternoon." Then he added, in a low voice, as they walked toward the cabin, "If I were you, Dix, I'd ask Carol to play Grandma Piggins's game, but if Sylvia's as horrid as I guess she is, it'll take a lot of 'magination to play it."

"Maybe Carol will. Anyway, I'll ask her," and, with a new hope in her heart, the little mother of them all entered the kitchen and began to dish up the porridge for the long-delayed breakfast.

But, try as the little mother might to be cheerful, the meal was a dismal one.

Baby Jim, usually so sunny, seemed to be affected by the doleful atmosphere, and suddenly began to sob as though his little heart would break.

[244]

"Dear me! Dear me!" poor Dixie sighed as she glanced across the room to where Sylvia sat in a miserable heap, her head hidden on her arms, silent now, except for an occasional sob that shook her frail body.

Up-stairs in the loft there was no sound, and Dixie wondered if Carol had covered her head with the quilt and was softly crying. How she longed to go up and comfort her, but she was needed just then in the kitchen.

Taking the small boy out of his high-chair, Dixie looked helplessly across the table at Ken, who was gulping down the porridge as though it were hard to swallow.

"Gee, Sis," he said, "what can be the matter with Jim? He's too little to understand. I don't see why he's crying so hard. Is there a pin pricking him, maybe?"

"No-o, that's one thing that couldn't happen," the girl answered with justifiable pride. "When he pulls a button off, I stop right that minute and sew it back on, so I never have to use pins." Then she added, "Once, when young Mrs. Jenkins spanked her baby just 'cause he was crying, Grandma Piggins said the best way to quiet a little fellow was to give him something pleasant to think about."

[245]

Then Ken had an inspiration. "I say, Jimmy-Boy," he began, leaning over and peering into the tear-wet face that was half hidden on Dixie's shoulder, "if you'll eat every spoonful of your milk and porridge, Big Brother will let you ride on Pegasus and hold the reins all by your very own self."

The dearest desire of the small boy was to reach that age when he would be considered old enough to sit, unsupported, upon the back of the gentle, jogging creature, hold the reins, and drive alone. Ken's offer had been an inspiration, for the little fellow's tears ceased, and his face, which Dixie kissed till it was rosy, beamed up at her with its sunniest smile. Then, once more in his high-chair, he fulfilled his share of the bargain by eating porridge to the very last mouthful.

Dixie glanced gratefully over at Ken, managing to say softly as she passed him on her way to the stove, "Stay very close to Pegasus when Jimmy takes his first ride, won't you?" Then she added, as she noted an expression of reproach in her brother's eyes, "Of course, Ken, I know that you would, anyway."

Five minutes later the two boys, hand in hand, went outdoors to feed the "live-stock," which consisted of a goat, Pegasus, the burro, Topsy and her kittens, the three little hens, and Blessing, the pig. As soon as the door closed behind them, Dixie went across the room and placed her hand on the bent head. "Sylvia," she said kindly, "won't you come to the table and have some breakfast?"

There was no response. The child curled up in the chair did not stir. Pity filled the heart of the older girl, and impulsively she knelt, and, putting her arm about the frail figure, she said tenderly: "Don't grieve so hard, Sylvia. Your father told me your mother is sure to get well. You can go home again in two short weeks."

Then the unexpected happened. The child lifted a face that was more angry than sorrowing, and sitting erect, she exclaimed vehemently, "I'm not crying about my mother. I'm crying 'cause I just hate my father. He'd no right to bring me to this poor folks' cabin. My mother told him I was to be put in a boarding-school where children from the best families go. My mother don't want me to associate with poor folks' families. O dear! O dear! What shall I do?"

The sobbing began afresh, but there was a chill in the heart of the older girl, who, almost unconsciously, held herself proudly. "Well," she said rather coldly, "since it's only yourself you are pitying, I wish your father had taken you somewhere else, but he didn't. He wanted you here with us, and so I suppose you will have to stay."

Then she asked hopefully, "Sylvia, couldn't you try to be happy here, for your father's sake, just two little weeks? Won't you try, dearie?"

"No, I won't!" the pale, spoiled child snapped without looking up. "And I'm not going to stay, neither."

Dixie sighed, and, turning, she started toward the ladder that led to the loft. Was Carol going to be as stubborn as Sylvia was, she wondered.

CHAPTER THIRTY-TWO
A HARD GAME

Dixie climbed the ladder to the loft and looked quickly toward the bed, but the little sister whom she sought was not there. Going to the curtained-off corner, she quickly drew aside the cretonne, and there, sitting on the floor, holding fast to the old doll for comfort and companionship, was Carol.

There were no tears in the beautiful violet-blue eyes that were lifted, but there was an expression in them so hurt that Dixie knew that it would be very hard for her little sister to forgive their unwelcome guest. Too, when she recalled the spoiled girl's rudeness of a moment before, Dixie suddenly resolved that she would not ask Carol to put herself in a position to be again humiliated as she had been in her recent experience in the Clayburn home.

[249]

"Dearie," she said, as she stooped and took the warm hand of the younger girl, "please come out of that dark, smothery place. I've thought of a plan, and I want to talk about it to you. First of all, I want you to be happy 'cause this is your home, not Sylvia's."

Carol smiled up gratefully and came out willingly. "Oh, Dix," she said, "what shall we do? I don't want to go down-stairs and have to see that mean-horrid girl. Won't you please send her away?"

Poor Dixie looked her despair, for, after all, she was very young herself, and this problem seemed too difficult a one for her to solve. They owed so much to kind Mr. Clayburn, they just couldn't turn his little girl out of their home, but what could they do with her in it?

"I 'most don't know what to do," she confessed, turning toward Carol a face that quivered sensitively. "I was wondering if, maybe, you'd like to go over to the Valley Ranch and visit. You know Sue's mother has often asked you to come. I didn't know but maybe you'd rather do that than stay here with Sylvia."

[250]

Carol pouted. "No, I don't want to leave my own home. If anybody's sent over to the Valley Ranch, I should think it ought to be Sylvia." The tone in which this was said was so reproachful that the perplexed girl could be brave no longer, and, throwing herself unexpectedly upon the bed, she sobbed as Carol had never heard her cry before. Feeling that she was in some way to blame, she ran to her side, exclaiming contritely: "Oh, Dixie, Dixie! Please don't cry that way. I'll do anything you say. I won't care if Sylvia slaps me even—if only you won't cry."

With a glow of happiness in her heart, the little mother of them all sat up, and, catching the younger girl in her arms, she held her close. It was such a comfort to her to know that Carol loved her and was willing to do something that would be, oh, so hard, to prove her love.

To show that she had really meant the hastily-made promise, the younger girl said, "Tell me what you want me to do, Dix, and I'll go right this minute and do it."

[251]

Then Dixie, sitting on the edge of the bed and holding fast to the little sister she loved, told her, as she had told Ken, about Grandmother Piggins's game of pretend. "It'll be awfully hard to pretend even to myself that I like Sylvia Clayburn," Carol said; "but I'll play that game, Dix, I will, honest, if you want me to."

"Goodie, let's start right this very minute," the older girl exclaimed. "Now, remember, we're to pretend that the horrid, rude things she will say are pleasant things."

The younger girl sighed as she replied, "Well, I like hard games, but this one will be the hardest that I ever played." Then, rising, she held out her hand as she continued, "Come on, Dixie, I'm going down to breakfast."

What a glad light there was in the plain, freckled face of the older girl, and, springing to her feet, she kissed her truly beautiful younger sister as she whispered: "Thank you, dearie, you have made me very happy. Now it won't be half so hard." Then they left the loft and went down the ladder together.

Carol, eager to please Dixie, upon reaching the kitchen at once looked about for the small visitor whom she was to treat just as though she really liked her. She soon spied the little figure curled up in the big rocker, and a feeling of real sympathy swept over the heart of Carol.

Sylvia was indeed to be pitied, for she did not have a big, brave brother like Ken, nor a wonderful sister like Dixie, nor an adorable Jimmy-Boy, and, although she did live in a much finer house, it was not a real home. But, more than all else, the pale, sickly, spoiled child was to be pitied because she had such a vain, foolish mother.

Although Carol did not think these things out, she nevertheless did feel sorry for the little girl who was as unhappy because she had to visit them as they were to have her, and she decided to make the ordeal easier for Dixie by doing her part in the pretend-game.

The elder girl went at once to the stove to reheat the porridge for her own and Carol's breakfast, but the younger little maid skipped across the room and said pleasantly: "Hello, Sylvia! You've come to visit us, haven't you? Did you bring your dollie?"

"No, I didn't!" was the sullen response. "You broke my best doll and I'm never going to forgive you. Never! Never!"

Now this was untrue, for it had been Sylvia's own carelessness that had broken the doll, as she very well knew.

The injustice of it was almost more than Carol could bear, and her natural inclination was to angrily retort and tell the unwelcome guest just how "mean-horrid" she really was, but that wouldn't be playing the game, and so, with a quick glance across at Dixie, who returned an encouraging smile, Carol silently repeated the formula which her big sister had suggested before they had left the loft: "What would I do or say if I *really* loved Sylvia?" What, indeed? How would Sylvia receive her advances? Would the spoiled little girl fly into a temper, or would she be kind?

With a long breath, the small girl said, "I'm sorry, Sylvia, if you really think that I broke your big doll. I wouldn't have done it, not for anything."

Then, as Dixie was serving the porridge, Carol asked, "Won't you come over to the table and have breakfast with us?"

"No, I won't," was the ungracious response. "I'm going to starve right here in this very chair, and then I guess my father will be sorry be brought me to this poor folks' cabin."

Dixie, hearing this cruel retort, glanced anxiously across at her little sister, whose cheeks were burning, while her violet-blue eyes flashed. Would she be able to play the game after that, the big sister wondered.

Six months before the small girl would have informed Sylvia that she was a descendant of James Haddington-Allen of Kentucky, who was "blue-blooded."

Before Carol could decide just how to reply, the sweet voice of her sister called her: "Come, dear, breakfast is ready! We'll keep the porridge warm, and Sylvia may have some nice rich cream and sugar on her share when she feels real hungry."

[255]

Then the two little Martin girls seated themselves at the table, and Carol felt well repaid for the effort she had made when she felt Dixie's hand clasp hers just for a moment. Anger left her heart. What did it matter what Sylvia said or thought since Ken and Dixie and Jimmykins loved her?

When breakfast was over, the boys returned from feeding the "live-stock," and then all was hurry and scurry while the little mother got them off to school. Their unwelcome guest had turned the big chair so that the high wooden back hid her from their view, but at the door Carol paused to call, "Good-by, Sylvia." There was no response from across the room, but Dixie caught her little sister and kissed her, whispering gratefully: "Thank you, dear. You are such a help." Then the door closed, and Dixie was left alone with the rebellious guest.

[256]

CHAPTER THIRTY-THREE
RUDE LITTLE SYLVIA

Dixie stood in the open door, watching the three children as they climbed the trail, and when they reached the top, before they turned into the cañon road, they waved back to her, and the little mother of them all smiled and nodded. Then she went into the kitchen with a sigh that she tried to change into a song. She noticed that the big chair had been turned, and that Sylvia was no longer curled up in it, but sat, leaning back, her thin legs hanging listlessly, for they were not quite long enough to reach the floor.

Sylvia looked so wan and miserable that Dixie silently asked herself the question that she and Carol had planned for the game: "What would I say and do if I really liked Sylvia?"

[257]

For a few moments she said nothing as she went about her morning tasks. Her thoughts were busy searching for an answer to her query, but it was hard to decide what would be best to do, since her former advance had been so rudely met.

Dixie went into the small lean-to room to make Ken's bed and Jimmy-Boy's crib. When she returned she found the blue eyes of the little guest watching her.

"I'm hungry," Sylvia said, in a tone of voice which implied that she was being much abused. "I want cake and cocoa."

"I am sorry, but we children always have porridge for breakfast, and we drink cold milk," Dixie said. Then, fearing that she had not been as gracious as a hostess, even an unwilling hostess, should be, she added: "You can have all the sugar you want on the porridge, and the cream is so good."

"Well, you may bring me some, but I won't promise to eat it," said the small girl condescendingly as she curled one thin leg under her and leaned back as though she intended to remain indefinitely in that comfortable chair.

[258]

The lines of Dixie's sweet mouth became firmer. "Dearie," she said in a tone which convinced the listener that she was in earnest, "if you wish breakfast, you must come to the table." Then more gently she added: "If you were sick and couldn't walk, I'd fetch it to you on a tray. But you can walk as well as I can, Sylvia."

The pale-blue eyes opened in unfeigned astonishment. "Why, I have always had my breakfast brought to me on a tray," she said. "Fanchon brings it."

"Of course you do, dearie, at home, where you have a maid to wait on you, but here we all wait on ourselves. There now, I've put your porridge in one of our prettiest kept-for-company dishes, and here's a pitcher of cream and the sugar. You may eat it when you are ready to come to the table. Now I'm going up to the loft to make our bed."

Two minutes later Sylvia heard a sweet, birdlike voice trilling overhead. Ten minutes later, when Dixie reappeared, the small guest was sitting at the table eating the delicious porridge and cream with hungry enjoyment.

[259]

"It's 'most as good as cake, isn't it?" Dixie said brightly as she sat by the window to mend. There was always something waiting for the little mother to patch or darn.

Sylvia rather grudgingly had to confess that the porridge was good, adding that the cream in Genoa wasn't so thick and yellow.

"Town cream never is, I guess," Dixie said. Then, that the conversation need not lag, she told about the recent arrival of the kittens.

The little hostess glanced sideways, and was glad to see an almost eager expression on the thin sallow face that was turned toward her. "I've never seen baby kittens!" Sylvia was saying. "I'd like to."

Dixie laid down her sewing. "If you've finished your breakfast, I'll show you all over our tiny ranch. We have three hens, too, and a piggie and a burro."

[260]

Together they left the house, and before many minutes had passed Sylvia was actually laughing, for the goat was kicking frolicsome heels up at them as the two little girls stood leaning over the rail fence that surrounded the small enclosure. After a time they visited the shed down near the apple-orchard, and Topsy was induced to come forth into the sunlight and show her babies, who blinked and winked, for their eyes had not been open very long, and they wabbled and tumbled down to the great delight of the town girl, who had never owned a pet.

"Oh! oh!" she exclaimed joyfully as she picked up the snow-white pussy that was growing whiter and fluffier and more lovable every day, "how I'd like to own this kitty-cat. Can I have it to take home with me to keep?"

Dixie hesitated, then she added: "I'm sorry, Sylvia, but I couldn't give Downy-Fluff away. Topsy belongs to me, but that little white kitty is Carol's. You may have the spotted pussy, if you want him."

Sylvia put the white kitten down and walked away as she said: "No, I don't want that one. I will tell my father to pay you for that white kitten if you don't want to give it to me."

[261]

Dixie flushed and bit her lips while she hurriedly asked herself the game question: "What would I say or do if I really loved Sylvia?"

Catching the hand of the child, who was beginning to sulk, the older girl exclaimed brightly: "Come on and see Pegasus. You may ride him if you wish."

The burro came across the barnyard when Dixie called, and nosed her pocket, hoping for a lump of sugar.

Sylvia actually clapped her hands with delight. "I've always wanted to ride on a pony, but mother was afraid I would fall. May I ride this cunning little horse? He's so small it wouldn't hurt me if I did fall off."

[262]

Willingly Dixie put the simple harness over the head of the mouse-colored burro, and then patiently, for a long hour, she walked around and around the house, leading while Sylvia rode. At last as it was nearing noon the little hostess, weary indeed, suggested that they go indoors and have their lunch, and afterwards, when Sylvia said she was sleepy, Dixie hung the hammock under the pines, and the unwelcome guest curled up in it, and, lulled by the wind in the trees, she was soon asleep.

Dixie wished that she, too, might rest, but with an added member in her family to feed, she set about baking, tired but happy because she believed that the "pretend game" was really progressing.

CHAPTER THIRTY-FOUR
THE YOUNG ENGINEER DREAMS

Carol and Jimmy-Boy returned alone from school, for Ken, with the book he had borrowed from "dear teacher" under his arm, had gone at once to the top of the low peak, and, having shaded his eyes from the glare of the sun that was low in the west, he looked toward the high mountain beyond. Then, as he did not find what he sought, he let his gaze wander slowly over the valley that was silvery with sand and sagebrush.

With a sudden whoop of joy, he leaped from the rock upon which he had been standing, and started running as best he could down the trail on the lake side of the low mountain, toward a column of wavering smoke which could be seen half a mile away, near a stream where small trout were plentiful. As he approached the place, the column of smoke died down, but he no longer needed its guidance for he had reached the rushing, bubbling mountain brook and was soon clambering up over the jagged rocks, pausing now and then to halloo. At first only a hollow echo replied, but soon he heard the voice for which he had listened.

"Hi-ho! Friend or foe?"

"Friend, I'll say!" Ken joyfully shouted as he scrambled over the remaining boulder, and found, as he had suspected, a fisherman standing on the brink of the stream casting a tempting fly. On the bank at the side of the young giant, lay at least two dozen of the shining trout that would be so delicious when fried.

"Shall I keep quiet?" the boy asked, his eyes sparkling as he looked at the catch, but the fisherman shook his head and drew in his line.

"No, sonny, indeed not. You have only a few moments to stay, for the days are short now. The darkness drops down almost as soon as the sun is set. So-ho, you have a book for me? A ponderous volume, indeed! Wells? Great! I'll enjoy reading that. How long may I keep it?"

"I—I don't know. I—I didn't ask teacher." Then the boy grinned as he seated himself astride a rock near one on which Frederick Edrington sat turning the pages of the book.

Looking up suddenly, the young engineer asked, "Why so merry?" Then, closing the volume, he queried with interest, "What did you tell your teacher about me?"

"I tried not to tell her any lies," Ken declared, "but I'm afraid she sort o' got the idea that you're a real old man, and, 'cause I said that you liked to read history, she took the notion that you're a hermit-professor, and that you're living up here to study out something, rocks or fossils, whatever that may be."

The young man, with hands folded behind his thick, waving chestnut-brown hair, laughed as he replied, "I'm glad she does, although I can't see quite how she can reconcile that image of me with the name of my choice."

[266]

"Oh, I know now!" cried the boy, springing up in his eagerness. "Miss Bayley thinks you're a very old man, 'most a hundred, who is a naturalist, and she wanted me to ask you if you'd like to have her new book on the snakes that inhabit these mountains."

"Indeed I would! It doesn't matter what—er—your teacher suggests sending to me, Ken, tell her I'll be delighted to have it." The boy, who, just to keep his hands occupied, had started whittling, looked up when his companion hesitated. Little did he dream that on the tip of Frederick Edrington's tongue had been "vision of loveliness," but, since only two days before the engineer had declared that he had never been in love, and never would be in love, he did not wish to awaken in the lad's mind even a suspicion of the real interest with which the "old hermit" regarded the young teacher. Rising, the fisherman selected twelve of the largest of the small trout. "Ken, old pal," he said, "would it be too much to ask you to take these to your teacher? I'd like to have her see them just as they are, with their glistening scales still on, but, when she has admired them, will you prepare them for her, that she may fry them for her supper?" The boy had also risen and his eyes were glowing. "Bet you, I will," he declared. "That'll be a jolly fine way for you to say thanks for the book." Then, after promising to return the following Saturday, the boy took up the string of fish, shook the big hand of the tall friend whom he so admired, and started, half-running, half-sliding down the trailless side of the mountain, turning back every few moments to wave to the young man who stood, with arms folded, watching until the lad disappeared over the crest of the lower mountain on the other side of which lay the small hamlet of Woodford's.

[267]

Then, reseating himself, Frederick Edrington again opened the big book. As he did so, a kodak picture fluttered to the ground.

With a heart thumping in a most disconcerting manner, the young man, who "never had been in love and never would be in love," stooped to pick it up.

"Queer now," he thought, as he gazed long at the beautiful face that smiled up at him. "Queer now, isn't it?"

[268]

A wind, rising with the setting of the sun and the cool rush of the waters, was all the reply that he heard, and feeling happier than he had in many a day, he returned to his camp.

[269]

CHAPTER THIRTY-FIVE
THE PRETEND-GAME

The sun had set, but the western sky above the mountains was a glory of radiant colors when Ken leaped upon the low porch in front of a small log cabin and knocked eagerly upon the closed door. Instantly it was opened, and Josephine Bayley, in a blue bungalow apron, appeared. Her face gladdened at sight of the small lad who was holding up a string of glistening fish.

"Oh, Ken, did you catch those for me?" The young woman took the proffered gift and held it up in the soft crimson light that reflected back from the other side of the cañon.

"No'm, teacher, 'twasn't me, though how I do wish it had been! It was-er— Oh, yes, Rattlesnake Sam caught them, and he said he'd like me to dress them after you'd seen how pretty they are with their scales on." For one panicky moment the small boy had forgotten his friend's assumed name, and he had been on the verge of saying "Mr. Edrington." What a narrow escape that had been! For a second he was hardly conscious that Miss Bayley was speaking, then he realized that she was asking him if the "old gentleman" had liked the book she had loaned him. "Oh, yes'm, teacher, Miss Bayley. Rattlesnake Sam, he said 'Great!' when he saw it, and—and he told me he'd like the snake book, too, if you'd loan it to him. I'm going up to his camp next Saturday, so I could pack it along then if you could spare it."

The girl-teacher laughed. "I can spare it all right until next spring. Since all of the snakes have hibernated for the winter, I can't get near enough to one to see if he looks like his picture." Then, at the small boy's suggestion, she gave him the string of trout and he at once began, in a manner that showed his skill, to prepare them for the frying-pan. "Won't you stay and share them with me, Ken?" the girl-teacher asked, really hoping that he would accept.

"Oh, no'm, thank you, I couldn't. Dixie will be expecting me back, and—and—we're sort of having trouble over at our house."

"Ken! Trouble?" anxiously. "Why didn't you tell me this afternoon and I would have gone to Dixie at once. I meant to ask you after school why my little leader-of-songs was absent, but you disappeared so quickly after the bell for dismissal rang that I could not, and then I looked for Carol, and saw that she and Jimmy-Boy were running for home as fast as his chubby legs could go. Tell me, dear, what is wrong? Can I help?"

Ken had finished preparing the small fish, and had placed them side by side on a platter that his teacher had brought out. He handed the dish to her, and having wiped his knife, he closed it before he replied.

"It's a queerish kind of trouble," he said. Then he told the story, beginning with Mr. Clayburn's great kindness to them, and ending with the favor which he had asked them to do for him. "Of course Dixie's right, she always is, but it's awful uncomfortable having some one in the house who won't speak pleasant when she's spoken to." Then the troubled expression vanished as the lad declared brightly, "I shouldn't wonder, though, if by now Dixie has won the game."

Miss Bayley looked puzzled. "What game, dear?" she inquired. The lad explained the pretend-game which Grandmother Piggins had originated when Sue had disliked her roommate. "That blessed old lady," the young teacher declared warmly. Then she added: "And that blessed sister of yours, too. Of course she has won the game, Ken, and I'll prophesy that you'll all be in school to-morrow with your guest. Please tell Sylvia Clayburn that the teacher of the Woodford's Cañon school will be so glad to have her, either as a visitor or as a pupil, just as she may prefer."

"Thanks, Miss Bayley, Dixie'll be powerful grateful to you for sending that message, and now I must be goin' along. It gets dark awful early, doesn't it? Good-by, teacher!"

The lad had not gone far through the deepening dusk when he heard a sweet voice calling after him, "Ken, do you think your old hermit would let me go fishing with him some day?"

"I'll—I'll ask him," was the lad's reply; then he raced off into the darkness of the cañon.

Here was a new problem, and one which the small boy might have realized was ahead of him. If his beloved Miss Bayley ever saw Frederick Edrington, she'd know he wasn't an "old hermit," and, worse than that, she'd know that Ken hadn't told the square-honest truth.

But he felt better when he recalled that the young engineer very much disliked girls, and so, of course, he would keep in hiding, and equally of course it would not be very long before he would leave the mountain country.

How Ken wished that he had never agreed to let teacher think that Mr. Edrington was so old. To be sure, he hadn't really told any lies. What he had said was that the man who had built the camp-fire had *said* that his name was Rattlesnake Sam, and Mr. Edrington *had* said that, and of course even teacher knew it was an assumed name. Then, when she had asked if the camper was old, Ken hadn't *said* he was old; he had replied that Rattlesnake Sam wasn't a hundred yet. But, after all, he hadn't been square-honest. He could hardly wait until Saturday to ask Mr. Edrington if he might tell teacher the whole truth.

When Ken neared the log cabin, he suddenly stopped and listened as though he were much surprised at what he heard. Surely that was Dixie singing, and Carol piping in at the chorus. Then, when the song was finished, there was a joyful clapping of small hands. What could it mean, he wondered. Ken had dreaded this home-coming, believing that he would find the girls both on the verge of tears after a long hard day of playing the pretend-game.

A bright light streamed out of the cabin window, beckoning the lad to approach. Before going around to the door, he glanced in, and was truly amazed at the pretty sight that he saw. His sisters were preparing the evening meal, Dixie at the stove and Carol placing on the table the best kept-for-company dishes. This, however, was not what amazed the boy, for he often beheld a similar scene when he returned home after dark. The unusual part of the picture was the small girl who sat on a low stool, holding two kittens, one snow-white and one spotted with black. The watchful mother-cat was lying on the bear-skin rug near by.

Ken actually blinked his eyes hard, and then opened them wide again to reassure himself that he was not dreaming. Could that smiling little girl be the disagreeable and unwelcome guest of but eight hours before? It was indeed Sylvia. She had awakened from her nap that afternoon greatly refreshed, and had been eager to again ride upon the mouse-colored burro. This time she had declared that she was not afraid to ride alone, and so the little hostess, after starting her down the road toward the apple-orchard, had returned to her task in the kitchen, but often she had looked out of the window, when Sylvia, with a merry halloo, had announced that she was returning.

[276]

So courageous did the small girl become that one time she had actually urged Pegasus to canter, and then, as she rode past the open door, her shout had been one of triumph. Dixie, skipping to answer the call, had been glad indeed to see that the pale face of their little guest was flushed with excitement and real pleasure. When at last Sylvia, weary but happy, had entered the kitchen, she had exclaimed, as she sank down in the big chair, "That was the best fun I ever had in my whole life!"

In the heart of Dixie there had been a prayer of gratitude because dear old Grandma Piggins's pretend-game had been such a success, but of this she said nothing. "I'm glad, dear," had been her quiet reply; "you may ride every day if you wish, while you are with us."

Then, when Carol came home from school, Sylvia had at once said that she wished she could have the snow-white kitten. Almost unconsciously Carol had asked herself the question, "What would I do if I really loved Sylvia?" In a burst of generosity which delighted as much as it surprised Dixie, the small girl replied almost at once, "You may have Downy-Fluff for your very own pussy if—if you'd like to."

[277]

Then the unexpected happened. The little guest, perhaps for the very first time in her short life, considered some one else's wishes. "Why, Carol Martin," she exclaimed, "your sister Dixie said you loved that pussy so much you wouldn't want to give it away."

"I do love Downy-Fluff," the other little girl had replied.

"Then why did you say that I could have her for keeps?" To the small girl who had never had an unselfish impulse, this act was incomprehensible.

"Because I want to make you happy, Sylvia," had been the quiet reply.

Then, before more could be said, Carol had announced that she was going out to the shed and bring Topsy and her pussy-babies into the cabin.

[278]

That had happened about an hour before the return of Ken, and during that hour there had been a brand-new emotion stirring in the heart of Sylvia Clayburn, which just before bedtime prompted the small girl to perform the first unselfish act of her eight years.

Ken was about to take Topsy and the kittens back to the shed when Sylvia, rising, went to Carol, and, holding out the snow-white kitten, said: "Here's Downy-Fluff. She wants you to cuddle her good-night." Then stooping, she picked up the less attractive pussy that was rubbing against her foot. Smiling at the astonished Carol, she said: "I'm going to have this one for my very own kitten. Dixie said I might, and anyway, I think Spotty's kind of lonesome, 'cause nobody loves her nor wants her, the way they do Downy-Fluff."

And Ken, listening, knew that his sisters had won the "pretend-game."

Miss Josephine Bayley was not at all surprised the next morning to see the four little Martins appear above the ridge of the cañon road. Carol and Dixie were trudging side by side, while Ken, with a stick in his hand, was walking beside the mouse-colored burro, on which rode no less a small personage than Sylvia Clayburn, whose thin, sallow face was beaming above the yellow curls of the four-year-old, who sat in front of her.

[279]

When the schoolhouse was reached, Ken lingered behind to tie the burro in a grassy spot, and Dixie, taking their guest by the hand, led her into the little log schoolhouse.

"Miss Bayley," she said to the young teacher, who at once approached them, "this is little Sylvia Clayburn. She thought she'd like to come just as company to-day. She'll be going back to Genoa in two weeks, so maybe that wouldn't be time to really start having lessons."

"We are very glad to have Sylvia with us as a guest or as a pupil, just as she prefers," Miss Bayley said, as she took the frail, claw-like hand of the child who had never been strong. "Carol, your seat is wide enough for two little girls, isn't it? I am sure that Sylvia would rather sit with you than be alone, wouldn't you, dear?"

[280]

To the surprise of the younger Martin girl, she found that she was actually pleased when Sylvia somewhat shyly nodded her head and slipped her hand trustingly into that of the other little maid. She no longer had to ask herself the pretend-game question, for she really did like their little guest, and she was even eager to have her for a seat-mate.

As usual the morning session began with singing, and the teacher said: "Now that it is nearly November, I am going to suggest that we begin to learn a Thanksgiving song. I have written the words on the board. I will sing it first, Dixie, that you may get the tune; then we will go over it all together."

The pupils read the poem aloud, that they might become familiar with the words that told the many simple things which small boys and girls had to be thankful for. Then the teacher sang it, first alone, later with Dixie. There was a lilting little chorus that even Sylvia soon could sing, and the girl-teacher smiled as she glanced down at her. It was plain to note that this new experience—for Sylvia had never before been in a school-room—was greatly interesting the little guest.

[281]

Then the reading-hour began and Miss Bayley suggested the much-loved story of Cinderella. Each pupil, sufficiently advanced, read two pages, and, as the special fairy-tale reader was passed about, it at last came to Carol. When that little maid was seated again, Miss Bayley smilingly said, "Perhaps our little guest will read a page to us."

No longer afraid, that small girl willingly read the story, with which she was familiar, and a flush of pleasure appeared in her pale face when the kind teacher said encouragingly, "You read very well indeed, Sylvia, just as though you were telling something that really had happened."

The old grandfather's clock was soon chiming ten, and then the pupils flocked out into the golden October day, where Sylvia, for the very first time in her short life, found herself actually playing games with children who were not from the best families.

Maggie Mullet caught her hand in a ring-around game, and at another time Sylvia actually chose Mercedes Guadalupe for a partner in a hide-and-seek game.

[282]

That noon found the small girl, whose chief diet had been candy and cake, so hungry that she gladly accepted the thick sandwich offered by Dixie, and ate it almost as ravenously as did Ken. It was during the lunch hour that Miss Bayley beckoned to Dixie from the open door of the log schoolhouse. Excusing herself, the glad-eyed little girl bounded away from the others, wondering what dear teacher had to tell her,—some plan, she was sure, for Carol's birthday "s'prise."

[283]

CHAPTER THIRTY-SIX
KEN'S TALK WITH TEACHER

A week passed, and what a week crowded with wonderful events it had been.

November came, in the same golden glory that October had gone out.

"Doesn't winter ever come to your mountain country?" the teacher asked Ken one day, and the lad, after searching the soft, hazy blue of the sky for a threatening cloud, shook his head. "There'll be winter enough soon, Miss Bayley," he said, as one who knew from the experience of having lived through fourteen of those blizzardous seasons. Then the lad was silent as he trudged along by the side of the young woman whom he so admired. It was Friday afternoon, and the boy was "packing" the books for teacher.

[284]

"A bright new penny for your thoughts, Ken," Miss Bayley suddenly exclaimed. They had reached her doorstep, and she held out her hand for the packet he was carrying.

The lad actually flushed. "I—er—I was wondering if—that is, I was hoping that somebody would be marryin' soon."

"Goodness, Ken!" said the young teacher, her eyes showing surprise. "I didn't suppose that small boys were ever match-makers. Is there any one around here who is contemplating matrimony? Sue Piggins is too young, isn't she? I have seen her driving on Sunday afternoon with Ira Jenkins of late, but—"

"Oh, no'm, Miss Bayley," the small boy hastened to say. "I wasn't thinking of Sue and Ira. Mis' Piggins wouldn't hear of her daughter marrying a blacksmith's boy. I—er—I was thinking of a rich girl in the South; I guess she lives there, and I was a-wishing as how she'd marry the Lord of Dunsbury."

After a puzzled moment, Josephine Bayley laughed merrily. "Boy," she said, shaking a finger at him, "you've been reading one of Mrs. Jenkins's yellow-covered novels. Mrs. Enterprise Twiggly tells me that the blacksmith's wife reads novels even while she pares potatoes or scrubs the floor, and there is always a rich girl marrying a lord in one of them."

[285]

Ken grinned rather sheepishly.

"I don't wonder that you think I'm loony, Miss Bayley," he acknowledged. "I—er was hoping that Rattlesnake Sam could come down from the mountains before the blizzards set in." Then, fearing that he would have to reveal his friend's secret if he said another word, he started to run back down the trail, calling over his shoulder: "Good-night, Miss Bayley. I'll see you at the party to-morrow. The girls are terribly excited."

[286]

"Gee," he thought, as he went more slowly after entering the dusk of the cañon that was caused by the sheltering pine-covered stone wall that shut out the sun, although it was still golden in the valley and on the far peaks. "I 'most spilled the beans that time. I'd hate awful to have Miss Bayley find out that Rattlesnake Sam isn't an old, old 'fossil,' whatever that may be. An' I'd hate to have Mr. Edrington think I couldn't keep his secret, but it came over me so all of a sudden that to-morrow will be November sixth, Carol's birthday, and last year we had an awful storm that day, though often the real blizzards don't set in till Christmas." Then, as he thought of something more joyful, he began to whistle. "Gee, but I'll sure be glad when the snow does come, for then Mr. Edrington's coming down to live with us, and hide up in our loft, if his aunt should prowl around trying to find him to make him marry that girl he doesn't want. Aunts are queer!" the lad continued to soliloquize as he sauntered along more slowly, swinging a stick he had cut from a tree as he passed. "There's our great-aunt now. Dixie says she's rich as anything, and that she lives in such a big house in the South that she could put four little children like us in it and not miss the room we'd take the least mite." Then, as he turned into the trail that led down toward their own picturesque log cabin, the boy's heart warmed with a sense of pride and ownership. "Far as I'm concerned," he decided, "I'd heaps rather live right here than I would with our mother's priggish Aunt Judith, even if she does own acres and acres, and live in a sort of a mansion with white pillars."

A moment later Dixie appeared in the open door for she had heard a familiar whistle and the tune was one they both loved— "Be it ever so humble, there is no place like home."

"Be careful, Ken, that you don't even hint about the party," the older girl whispered. "Carol hasn't an inkling of an idea, and we want to s'prise her."

CHAPTER THIRTY-SEVEN
CAROL'S BIRTHDAY S'PRISE

"Happy birthday!" Dixie cried the moment that she was sure that the pretty violet eyes of her sister were really open.

"Oh, goodie! I'm nine years old to-day. Sylvia, are you awake?" Carol then called to the little guest who was sleeping on a cot bed in another part of the big loft room over the kitchen of the log cabin.

That small maiden sat up and nodded. Although she was still thin, a remarkable change had taken place in the one week that she had lived with "poor folks." She actually looked interested and happy, and there was a flush in the sallow cheeks, for even in seven days plenty of porridge and cream, hours of riding on the mouse-colored burro, and no candy and cake had begun to transform her from a sickly, spindling child to one who, were the pleasant simple ways continued, would soon be rosy and robust.

"Happy birthday, Carol," Sylvia called gleefully. Then she added. "There's a s'prise coming to-day."

"Oh, goodie, what is it?" The younger of the Martin sisters was already dressing, for Dixie had said that "whatever you do on your birthday you will do all the year," and so great had been the change in Carol that she now actually wished to be down-stairs in time to help her older sister prepare breakfast.

Ten minutes later they were all in the kitchen. Carol's pretty face was flushed with excitement. "If there's a s'prise for me," she said, "why can't I have it now?"

The others shook their heads. Ken, who had come in with a pail brimming with creamy milk, looked up at the clock, and then began to count. "Oh, it's hours and hours before the real surprise is to begin," he said to tease.

[290]

"But I can't wait hours and hours. I just can't. I'll burst with curiosity! I know that I will," the small girl declared as she brought Baby Jim from his crib and began to dress the little fellow.

Only a few months before, as Dixie could easily recall, this same little maid had pouted and felt very much abused if she had been asked to perform this loving service for her small brother. What gratitude there was in the heart of the little mother of the brood that glorious sixth of November.

Ken was straining the milk. Sylvia was setting the table. "Let's use the best kept-for-company dishes all day," Dixie said. "Birthdays are very special."

This was done. Then, while the five children sat about the board, eating the porridge and cream, on which bananas had been sliced to make it "extra better," as Ken declared, Carol began to tease first one and then another. "Sylvia," she accused, "I know, by a sort of laughing look in your eyes, that you know just what the s'prise is to be."

"Of course she knows, and so do we all," Dixie put in, "but we won't any of us tell, not until the clock strikes two. Then it's going to happen."

[291]

Carol clapped her hands. "Oh! Oh! It's something that's going to happen, is it?" Then, whirling unexpectedly and facing her big brother, she challenged: "Ken Martin, I never knew you to tell a lie in your whole life, and so I'm going to ask you. Is the surprise going to happen here in this house?"

"Don't you tell, brother," Dixie warned.

The laughing lad sprang up. "I'm off for the Valley Ranch. Won't be back till lunch." Then, seizing his hat, he darted away, stopping in the door to say, "Now, if Carol finds out, it won't be from me."

Such a merry morning as those three girls had. Jimmy-Boy was too young to understand what the laughter and bantering was all about. At last lunch was over; Ken had returned, and the excitement in that old log cabin was tense, for the two older Martins and their guest were preparing for the surprise trying all the time to hide even the simplest of these preparations from the curious gaze of the one most interested.

[292]

At last it was half-past one and time to dress. The three small girls had climbed the ladder to the loft, and Dixie looked often at her small sister, who was donning the very best gingham and buttoning it down the front. Now and then the violet eyes glanced across the room to where Sylvia Clayburn stood arrayed in her pretty pink silk dress, but the sigh of yearning that arose to Carol's lips was quickly changed to a song.

Tears sprang to the eyes of the little mother, and, kissing the flushed cheek of the small girl who was nine that day, she said softly: "Carol, dearie, how long and beautiful your curls are this year. They hang almost down to your waist now, and they're so shimmery and silky."

The younger sister, knowing that Dixie was trying to help her count her blessings, smiled up beamingly, and little Sylvia crossed the room, and, taking one of the truly beautiful curls in her frail hand, she said: "You'd ought to be so happy 'cause you have them, hadn't she, Dix? My hair looks as though the color'd been all washed out, and it's straight as anything."

[293]

Carol glanced at the head of her little friend. The pale yellow hair wasn't a bit pretty, but Dixie was saying: "Sylvia, don't you mind a thing about it yet. Lots of times hair grows darker. I've heard Sue Piggins say that hers was nearly like yours when she was eight and now look at it, a heap of sunny gold."

"Somebody's driving in," Carol exclaimed. "Who do you suppose it is?"

"Go down and see," Dixie suggested.

The smaller girl, having heard the clock strike two, was sure that the "s'prise" was about to take place, and so she scrambled down the ladder that led from the loft to the kitchen. Skipping to open the door, she beheld on the porch no less a personage than Miss Josephine Bayley, and with her was Sue Piggins, while behind them loomed a tall youth who was Ira Jenkins, the blacksmith's good-natured, very shy, and much-overgrown son.

[294]

Miss Bayley held out both hands and kissed Carol first on one cheek and then on the other. "Happy birthday, dear," she exclaimed, "and may you have many more, and all as happy as I am sure that this one is."

The flushed little girl looked up at the young teacher with glowing eyes. "Oh! Oh!" she cried, "Now I know what the s'prise is. It's a party!" She whirled to find Dixie, Sylvia, and Ken standing back of her in the big sunny kitchen. Jimmy-Boy was taking his nap.

The older sister nodded. "That's part of the surprise," she began, when the awkward Ira stepped forward and handed Carol a long, flat box, as he said, "Here's 'nother part of it."

How the violet eyes sparkled. "It's a present, I do believe!" the small girl cried. "Oh, Dix, do see, here's a box with a present in it. Who do you 'spose it is from?"

"Open it and see," her sister, who was trembling with excitement, suggested. This was a wonderful hour for Dixie, an hour long dreamed of, but one that she had sometimes feared would never come true.

[295]

Carol was so eager that her small fingers just could not untie the strings, and so Ken sprang forward and offered the services of the two-bladed knife of which he was so proud.

Snap! Snap! The cord was sundered. Then Carol was about to lift the cover, when Dixie laid her hand on her sister's. "Guess first, what's in it," she suggested, wishing to prolong the thrilling moment.

"I say, Dix, that isn't fair," Ken interceded. So the small girl was permitted to lift the top and peep into the folds of soft tissue paper.

As she gazed at her very first blue silk dress, those who loved her were amazed to see that she grew very pale, then tears rushed into her lovely violet eyes, and, turning to her older sister, she threw her arms about that small girl and sobbed as though her heart would break.

"Why, why, Carol, are—are you disappointed, dear? Isn't it the color you've been wanting?" Dixie felt as though she, too, would have to cry, but the younger girl lifted her head and smiled through her tears. "I'm crying 'cause I'm so glad, glad, glad! There's lace in the neck and sleeves, just the way I've always wanted, and there's ruffles!"

How every one laughed, and then Sylvia spied a card in the silken folds.

This she pounced upon, handing it to Carol. "I know it!" that shining-eyed maiden exclaimed. "It's a gift from Dixie and from dear teacher."

Then it was that Ira remembered something, and darted out of the house and back to the buggy.

Dixie, the little mother of the brood of Martins, knew just why Carol had cried, for when the second box was opened, and in it was found a silk dress, the shimmery green of springtime, she felt as though she, too, would cry. She said little, although her wonderful gold-brown eyes were eloquent.

Miss Bayley went with her to the loft to help her don her new dress, and when they reappeared, the others actually stared, for Dixie looked almost pretty. In fact, Ken, as he glanced about at the guests, thought that, in some way he couldn't just describe she was the best-looking girl there.

Miss Bayley saw it, too, that something in the face they had called plain, which seemed to prophesy that the young lady who-was-to-be would be called beautiful. Perhaps it was the glow of happiness which was making the little hostess so radiant; perhaps it was the new way that dear teacher had combed the red-gold hair, which, when loosened from its tight braid, waved and curled in little ringlets above her ears. Moreover, for the very first time, her head was adorned with a witching big, pale-green, butterfly bow. On Carol's curls was another like it, only it was the color of the sky in June.

Ken had disappeared, though no one had noticed it. Suddenly there came a tapping on an outer door, and when Sylvia, being nearest, skipped to open it, in walked Topsy with a red bow around her neck, while Spotty and Downy-Fluff followed, wearing smaller neck-ribbons.

Ken, who had been hiding for a moment, bounded in after them, grinning his delight as he said, "I thought maybe the kits would like to come to the party, and if I'd had a pink ribbon, I'd have brought Blessing in, too."

"Goodness! I'm glad you didn't have," Sue exclaimed. "I've been brought up with pigs, but I don't like them, even yet, leastwise not for pets."

Sylvia seemed to be watching for some one. Every few minutes she would run to the window and look up toward the cañon road.

"I wonder if she's 'spectin' a s'prise, too?" Carol said softly to Dixie. That little maid declared that she didn't know what Sylvia was watching for. Then, at Miss Bayley's suggestion, games were played, such as hide-the-thimble and drop-the-handkerchief. When every one was laughing and shouting with interest and excitement, there came a loud knocking at the door.

Sylvia put her hand on her heart and cried, "Oh! Oh! I do believe it's come, and I had forgotten to watch."

She leaped to open the door, and the others crowded round, wondering what they were to see. It was no less a personage than Mr. Hiram Tressler, the stage-driver.

"Howdy!" he began, his leathery face wrinkling in a pleasant smile. "This here's one of the boxes, Miss Clayburn, but the other one that yer pa sent over is too heavy for me to cart down the trail all alone. Maybe now Ken and Ira'd better come up and help me h'ist it out o' the stage."

"It's a birthday present from me."

The boys sprang forward with alacrity, and followed the old driver back up the steep trail. While they were gone, Sylvia, her face flushed with pleasure, handed a long, narrow box to Carol. "It's a birthday present from me," she said.

In that box was the most beautiful doll that the little girl had ever seen. "Why, it's prettier even than the one that—that—" Carol could say no more, but turned tear-brimmed eyes toward the giver of the treasured gift.

Joy shone in Sylvia's pale-blue eyes. It was the first time that she had ever known the great happiness of giving a present to some one. Impulsively she stepped forward, and, kissing the girl who was holding the doll in her arms, she said softly: "Carol, I've been just mean and horrid. I knew all the time that you didn't break my dolly, and—and I asked Papa to get this one for your birthday. I'm sorry, and—and I love you now, just like you were a really, truly sister."

[300]

They were too young to know that this love was the greatest gift that was given to Carol on her ninth birthday.

"What do you s'pose the boys went to get?" Sue Piggins was peering out of the door and up toward the trail as she spoke.

"I don't know. I didn't 'spect Mr. Tressler to bring anything more'n just the box with the doll in it, and that's here," Sylvia said as she, too, peered out curiously.

"The stage is driving up the cañon," Sue reported to the others in the living-room, "so maybe it wasn't anything for us after all." But Sylvia's sharp eyes caught sight of the two big boys who were coming slowly down the trail, carrying something between them. "Oh! Oh! I know!" she cried excitedly. "It's ice-cream in a freezer!"

[301]

Mr. Clayburn had sent it, and since Sue had brought a wonderful frosted cake as a gift from her mother, Dixie at once laid out the best kept-for-company dishes, and refreshments were served. An hour later, when the guests departed, Ken went with them to help dear teacher into the buggy. He looked up at her with shining eyes. "Oh, gee-whizzle, look't the sky, Miss Bayley!" he exclaimed. "I do believe a blizzard's coming. How I do hope 'tis!"

Miss Bayley looked her surprise. "Why, Ken," she said, "how strange! Do you honestly want this glorious autumn weather to turn into a blizzard?"

"Yes'm, that is, I—er—I mean I'd like to have Rattlesnake Sam come down from the mountains and pay us a visit," the lad stammered, growing red as though he were embarrassed.

Ira was starting the horses and so Miss Bayley said no more, but she was puzzled, and wondered if anything had happened to the imagination of her best pupil in mathematics.

[302]

CHAPTER THIRTY-EIGHT
THE EXPECTED BLIZZARD

The threatening blizzard broke over the Sierra Nevadas about sundown, and for three days it raged. Ken seemed to be hilariously excited, and Dixie, Carol, and Sylvia wondered about it. The snow, which had commenced falling the first night, did not cease, and had it not been that the lad worked untiringly with a shovel, the animals and hens would have been without food.

At last Dixie suggested that the lean-to shed, which was back of the kitchen, should be occupied by the three hens, the small pig, and the goat.

"Topsy and the two kittens can come in with us. I always make her a bed back of the stove when the winter storms come," the little mother explained to Sylvia.

[303]

"But what shall you do with Pegasus?" that small maiden asked.

That was indeed a problem. "We didn't have our burro last winter," Dix said. Then she added, "What *shall* we do with him, Ken? When the snow piles up half-way to the top of the house, you can't keep a path shoveled out to the barn. We'll just have to bring Pegasus in somewhere."

The lad rubbed his ear, which was stinging with the cold, for he had but recently come in from the storm. "I dunno," he finally conceded, "unless we put him in the lean-to shed and tie him up in one corner. Then we can sort of fence off the three other corners and put the goat in one and the hens in the other, and Blessing in the last."

[304]

How Sylvia laughed. "I never had so much fun before in all my life," she confessed. Monday came and although the storm was not raging quite as furiously as it had been, still the four children could not attempt to go to school, nor did Miss Bayley expect them. Ken was very restless, and kept listening, as though he expected to hear some sound besides the moaning and whistling of the wind. Too, he would stand for fifteen minutes at a time straining his eyes through the dusk, watching, watching up the trail.

"Ken Martin, you act so queer!" Carol said at last. "Whatever are you looking out of the window for? You've seen the ground covered with snow lots of times before, haven't you? Come on over here and help us tease Dixie to let us make some popcorn balls."

[305]

The boy turned reluctantly back into the room, and, at the suggestion of his older sister, he brought forth a few ears of corn, which the laughing "twins," as they now called Sylvia and Carol, began to shell. Then he procured the old-fashioned, long-handled popper, and five minutes later he was shaking this over a bed of red coals in the stove. The little town girl, who had never seen corn popped, stood with an arm about her best friend, watching with great interest. The kernels were bursting merrily into downy white puffs when Ken suddenly stopped shaking and listened intently. There was a prolonged dismal whistle of the wind down the chimney. That was all the girls heard, but Ken was sure that he had heard something else. "Here, Dix," he said, as he held the handle of the popper toward her, "you take this. I want to go outside and listen." The oldest girl complied, and the lad, putting on his heavy cap and coat, and lighting his lantern, opened the door. A gust of cold wind and sleet swept into the kitchen. Carol and Sylvia sprang to push the door shut, and, as they did so, the wide flame in the kerosene lamp flickered as though it would go out, but a moment later it steadied and shone on the puzzled faces of the three little girls.

"Dix," Carol said, "brother's been acting awfully queer of late, don't you think so? He seems to be expecting somebody, and yet who in the world could it be? There's nobody coming to visit us, is there?"

[306]

The older sister smiled. Ken had thought best to take her into his confidence, since he had offered the loft to his friend. She had assured him that he had done the right thing, but she did hope that Ken's friend would not come until Sylvia had returned to Genoa. The little housekeeper didn't know how they would all find places to sleep, but she remembered that Grandmother Piggins had often said, "Don't step over a stile till you come to it."

The corn had been popped till it filled a big yellow bowl, but Ken had not returned. Dixie carried the lamp to the window nearest the cañon trail. She was sure that she saw the lantern far off among the pine trees, but, as she watched, it disappeared. Then a sudden blast of wind roaring past the cabin told her that the storm was again increasing in fury. Why didn't Ken come in, she wondered. Perhaps an uprooted tree had pinned him under. Perhaps she ought to go and find him.

When she arrived at this decision, she placed the lamp on the table by the window and went quietly to the loft to get her heavy coat and hood.

[307]

When Dixie ran out of the log cabin into the storm which was increasing in fury, she was at first so blinded by the stinging snow that she could see nothing. Then, when she had pulled her hood down in a way that sheltered her eyes, and had gathered the folds of her cloak tightly about her, she stood on the narrow path which Ken had shoveled a few hours before, and gazed through the dense blackness up toward the cañon road.

Again she saw a glimmer of light, as though it might be a lantern. Was Ken swinging it, hoping to attract her attention?

Believing that she had guessed aright, the small girl began battling the elements, and slowly she ascended the trail that led to the road. Now and then she stumbled over covered rocks, and at last reached the deep, unbroken snow, for Ken had not tried to shovel a path up the steep trail to the highway, and his own foot-prints had been hidden quickly by the storm.

[308]

Luckily the dim light of the lantern appeared again, and the girl headed directly for it. During a lull, she was sure she heard her brother call. After all, she feared that her surmise, that a falling tree had pinned him down, was correct, otherwise he surely would have returned to the cabin. It was at least half an hour since he had started out in search of he knew not what.

She stood still once more and listened. Again she heard the sound, and this time she knew it was her brother hallooing.

"Ken! Ken!" she shouted. "I'm coming! I'm 'most there!"

Then, as she paused to listen, she was sure that she heard an answering cry, though it seemed faint and far. Breaking through a dense growth of dwarf pines, to her great joy she saw, in a circle of light from the lantern a short distance above her, the erect form of a boy, which proved to her that at least her brother was unhurt. But as she hastened forward, she saw him lean over something that looked like a log. The girl knew that it must be the figure of a man. "Oh, Ken," she cried as soon as she was near enough to be heard, "who is it out in all this blizzard?"

[309]

"It's Mr. Edrington. He 'twas that was hallooing when I first heard a call. He had to leave camp, for his shelter blew away, and he couldn't make a fire, for the matches were all wet. He tried to find the easy trail down the mountain, but the snow had covered it. He missed the way and fell right over the cliff. He's got grit all right, Mr. Edrington has! He sort of dragged himself here. When I came, though, he'd petered all out, but he told me that much before he—he—"

The girl had knelt on the snow, and was listening to the man's heart. "It's only a faint he's in," she said, looking up at the lad. "If we rub his face and hands with snow, perhaps it will help him to come to."

"Dix, you're a brick!" the boy exclaimed admiringly. Then hopefully they did as the girl had suggested, watching anxiously the pale face upon which the light of the lantern shone. The wind had subsided, as it did periodically, and there was a strange silence under the pine trees. Too, the moon appeared through a rift in the clouds, making a beautiful picture of the wide, glistening cañon, while near by, the pine branches bent low under the weight of gleaming snow.

The young engineer slowly opened his eyes.

[310]

To the great relief of the boy and girl the young engineer slowly opened his eyes; then he looked about with a puzzled expression. Seeing Ken, he smiled. "I say, where am I, old man?" he asked. Turning, he saw Dixie, and he sat up as though startled.

"It's only my sister, Mr. Edrington," Ken explained. "She's grown a lot since you saw her last."

"Of course," the young man laughed as he took the girl's hand. "I must have been dreaming. I thought you were Marlita Arden. Oh, I remember now. I fell over the cliff, didn't I? Wonder if any bones are broken. Give a lift, Ken, and I'll soon find out."

With the aid of the strong boy and girl, the stalwart young man stood on his feet, and was indeed pleased to find that he could walk without pain.

However, he quickly put his hand to his head.

"That's where I hit when I landed, I guess," he said, trying to speak lightly. He staggered as he walked, and was glad indeed when the cabin was reached and he found himself lying on Ken's bed in the small room adjoining the kitchen.

Carol had put another stick on the fire and had filled the teakettle. Dixie praised her small sister for her thoughtfulness. How glad, glad, that little mother was when she realized that Carol was beginning to think of others.

As the older girl prepared a hot beverage for their unexpected guest, she was wondering where her brother would sleep. Surmising this, the lad told her he'd fold a quilt and sleep on the floor near the stove. "Ira and I slept on the hard ground for a week when we were off wood-cutting for his dad," he concluded.

Dixie went to bed that night with a strange feeling—a premonition perhaps—that something unusual was about to happen. Nor was she wrong.

CHAPTER THIRTY-NINE
A HAPPY FATHER

The next day dawned gloriously, but the snow was still too deep in the cañon for the children to attend the morning session of the log-cabin school.

"The snow-plow will be along soon, I suppose," Carol said, as she peered up toward the highway.

Sylvia, who stood at Carol's side exclaimed: "Look! Look! There's a shining white cloud flying low. Did you suppose clouds ever came so far down the mountain?"

Carol gleefully clapped her hands. "It's the plow going up the road this very minute," she cried in joy. "It throws up the snow in clouds just like that." Then she added: "I'll tell my brother. He'll want to finish shoveling our path now."

"Oh-ee! How I'd love to help shovel," Sylvia exclaimed. "Couldn't you and I help, Carol?"

"Of course we could, and maybe it would be kind of fun! We haven't been out of the house for 'most four days. I'll ask Dixie."

The older girl thought the plan a splendid one, and she bundled up Jimmy-Boy, that he might accompany them. With the three children away from the cabin, Mr. Edrington might get the undisturbed sleep that he so needed to restore his strength.

The younger girls climbed to the loft and put on their leggings, rubbers, and heavy coats and hoods; then, getting small shovels, they joined the boy who was already working with a will, his cheeks the color of the muffler that was tied about his neck.

When they were far enough away from the cabin to shout, without being heard by the injured man, they paused now and then in their path-making to have a snowball battle, and, at last, when they had cleared the trail to the highway, the four children stood looking admiringly at the road that had been so recently smoothed by the snow-plow.

Suddenly Ken sang out, "Hark, what do I hear?"

"Sleigh-bells, I do believe," Carol cried.

"Jingle! Jingle! Somebody's coming. Let's guess who." Sylvia, her cheeks flushed, her eyes sparkling, watched the bend in the road expectantly. "I'll guess it's Mr. Piggins," she concluded.

"I'll guess it's—" Ken began, but before he could mention a name, a trim little cutter, drawn by a spry white horse, appeared.

There was a cry of joy from one of the children.

"It's my dad! My dear, dear dad!" Leaping from the trail into the highway, Sylvia waved her red-mittened hand, laughing and shouting. The man in the rapidly-approaching sleigh looked at the small girl as though he could not think who she might be.

Then with an expression of radiant gladness, he called "Whoa!" tossed the reins to Ken and held out his arms to catch the small figure that was flying toward him.

"My Miggins!" the father's voice was tender with emotion. "This can't be you!"

He held her off at arm's length to gaze at her with admiring eyes.

The small girl laughed up at him happily, her eyes bright, her cheeks as rosy as Carol's. Then again holding her close, he said softly: "Little girl, your mother is at home now, and she wants to see you. She has been asking every day since the storm set in if I wouldn't go and get her baby for her." Then he added anxiously: "Are you old enough, I wonder, to see the great change that there is in your mother, and not let her know? Our loved one is very frail yet, little daughter, but I believe, when you are with her, she will be more content and will grow stronger again. We will try to help her, for she longs to get well, that she may enjoy the simple home life which, somehow, we have always missed." Then, smiling down at the other three children, the genial banker called, "Pile in, all of you, and I'll give you a sleigh-ride."

Up they scrambled, stowing the shovels away as best they could. Then again the horse started, turning down the drive toward the cabin. How the sleigh-bells rang, and how the children shouted! Jimmy-Boy was most hilarious of all, and he wanted to keep on riding, even when Dixie appeared to lift him out and carry him into the warm kitchen. "I want more sleigh-ride," the little fellow kept saying. Then Dixie had an inspiration. "Maybe big brother will be able to make a bob-sled, and maybe Pegasus will pull it, and then Jimmy can go riding."

"Will there be a ting-a-ling?" The small boy had been about to cry, but he waited to hear his big sister's reply. Dixie hesitated. She never liked to promise anything that she could not grant.

"What's the matter with that little man?" the kind banker asked as he entered the kitchen.

Jimmy-Boy, from his place on Dixie's lap, hastened to tell him. "I want ting-a-ling to put on Pegthus."

Mr. Clayburn looked so truly mystified that Dixie had to explain that Pegasus was their burro, and that the little fellow wished they had a string of bells to put about his neck.

[317]

"A splendid suggestion!" the genial man exclaimed. "I was wondering what I could do with the old bells, now that I have bought a new harness. Pegasus shall have them. Come with me, little chap, and we'll see how your burro likes them."

Ken accompanied them to the barn while Dixie went up to the loft where she found the two smaller girls busily packing the suit-case which Sylvia had brought with her.

That little maid stood up, and, throwing her arms about Dixie's neck, she said: "Oh, I just don't know how to tell you what a nice time I've had. How I do hope that I can come again!"

"Of course you'll come again—lots and lots of times," Dixie assured her.

Ten minutes later they were all out on the porch. Mr. Clayburn took the hand of the oldest girl as he said earnestly, "Dixie, I shall never be able to repay you four little Martins for all that you have done for my small daughter, but promise that you will call on me if ever you need help in any way."

[318]

Dixie was glad to promise. Then, when the sleigh had been driven away, Ken said: "I didn't tell Mr. Clayburn the reason for Mr. Edrington's being here. That's his secret. He doesn't want any one to know."

"Nobody shall know!" Dixie promised, but she was mistaken.

[319]

CHAPTER FORTY
A MYSTERY SOLVED

Miss Bayley could not understand why the Martin children did not come to school that afternoon, for she had seen the snow-plow pass by and knew that the road was open. So anxious did she become that she dismissed the three pupils who were there, at two o'clock. Then, donning her warm wraps, she started walking down the highway toward the cañon.

The air was clear and sparkling. The girl-teacher felt as though she could run and shout, as the children did, but, fearing that she might shock Mrs. Enterprise Twiggly, she waited until she was on the downward trail and out of sight of the inn, then she flung her arms wide and sang a glad song of her childhood.

"Oh, but it's good to be alive!" she said as she turned into the narrow, well-shoveled trail leading to the cabin. Just then a breeze, on mischief bent, perhaps, tossed a heavily-laden pine bough above her head and a small avalanche of snow crashed down upon her. Laughingly, she shook herself as best she could.

The snow had knocked her cherry-colored tam awry, and had loosened her hair, which curled at the ends and clustered about her ears and on her neck. With cheeks flushed and eyes brimming with mirth, the girl-teacher tapped upon the door of the cabin. No one answered, and she pushed it open and found herself facing a strange young man who, wrapped well in blankets, sat in the big easy-chair close to the stove. How Frederick Edrington had longed to climb to the shelter of the loft when he had seen the unwelcome guest passing the window, but there had not been time.

For one terrorized moment he had feared that, when the door opened, he would behold either his aunt or the dreaded Marlita Arden. It was with an audible sigh of relief that he beheld the vision of his dreams.

Miss Bayley was the more startled of the two. "Oh!" she exclaimed, as she backed toward the door again. "I—I didn't know that the Martin children had company. I am so sorry—if—if I—" she hesitated.

The young man was the first to recover his presence of mind. "You haven't, Miss Bayley," he said with the smile that won friends for him among rich or poor, young or old. "I assure you that you have done the very nicest thing that you possibly could have done. I'm mighty glad to see you again. I—"

"Again?" The girl-teacher was indeed surprised, and at once began to search her memory for the time of their former meeting. Surely she could not have forgotten the good-looking young man, who bronzed face, with its clear-cut features, plainly told that his life-work kept him out-of-doors.

"Pardon me for not rising, Miss Bayley, and please do slip off your cloak and stay a while," he begged. "Dixie and the others have gone to the Valley Ranch on an errand, but they will soon return."

[322]

Then, as he saw the puzzled expression in her eyes, the young man answered her unspoken query. "Miss Bayley, you have never met me before, but I have heard my little friends speak of you so often that I feel well acquainted with you."

Relieved, Josephine slipped off her fur-lined cloak and seated herself. For a moment she sat looking thoughtfully out of the window toward a snow-covered range that formed the other side of the wide cañon.

"May I hear about it?" the young engineer asked.

The girl smiled. "I was thinking of a queer old man who is camping up in the mountains, and wondering how he has weathered the storm."

"Oh, indeed!" Mr. Edrington sat up as though interested. "Is this—er—old man of whom you speak a particular friend of yours?"

The girl nodded, then laughed. "Well, at least I do feel friendly toward him because he likes books. He has had two of mine, one on snakes and the other a history."

[323]

Then, turning she asked a direct question: "Won't you tell me your name? It's hard to talk to a person and not call him anything."

The young engineer flushed. "I say, Miss Bayley," he apologized, "you'll think I'm a regular boor, won't you? I—er—my name is—Rattlesnake Sam."

The girl's amused laughter rang out, and though the listener was relieved, he was certainly puzzled.

"I was sure of it!" she said triumphantly. "You see what an excellent detective I am."

"But, I say, Miss Bayley, this isn't very complimentary. I do know that I need shaving, but Ken led me to believe that you thought Rattlesnake Sam was an old, dry-as-dust professor, a sort of 'fossil,' and I—er—" Then the young engineer laughed in his hearty, boyish way. "Honestly, Miss Bayley, I didn't suppose I looked quite that old and fogyish." Then the query: "Do I?"

[324]

The girl shook her head, but her eyes still twinkled. "No-o!" she confessed almost reluctantly, "and I'm dreadfully disappointed in you. I was actually looking forward to meeting the snake professor who looked like—well, like Thoreau or Burroughs, as I fancied, and now—" Pausing, the girl tilted her head sideways and gazed at him critically and yet merrily.

His good-looking bronzed face was expressive as he watched her, and his eyes were telling how much he admired her. He wondered what she would say.

"I believe I am disappointed in you," the girl declared, and yet in a tone that did not quite carry conviction. "You're much too modern to be real interesting."

The young man looked disconsolate. "Alas!" said he. "Fate seems to be against me." He glanced up hopefully. "I might grow a very long beard, Miss Bayley, if that would help to make me less modern and more interesting." Then, as she only laughed her reply, the young engineer continued. "But you haven't told me what clues you possessed that led you to discover my supposed well-hidden identity."

Josephine looked at him searchingly. "Can men keep a secret?" she inquired.

[325]

"Much better than boys can, or so I'm beginning to think," was the reply.

"No, you are wrong," Miss Bayley defended. "Ken didn't really tell. In fact, he doesn't know that he told at all. As I look back now upon our conversations concerning the old man in the mountains, I realize that Ken did his very best to keep your secret, but he said such strange things sometimes. He hasn't told,—not one word,—but one day when I offered him a penny for his thoughts, he said he was wishing somebody would get married, and he seemed so doleful about it that my curiosity was aroused.

"Then, when I told him that I thought he was rather young to be a match-maker, he confessed that what he was really wishing was that there would be a blizzard, so that his friend Rattlesnake Sam would have to leave the mountains and come down and stay at their cabin.

"Well, the storm did come and so, too, did you. Wasn't the inference a natural one?"

[326]

The young man nodded. "It wouldn't take a Sherlock Holmes to unravel that mystery," he began, and then paused, for he was sure the little ripple of laughter that he heard was prefacing a merry remark. Nor was he wrong, for Josephine continued: "There is one part, however, that I cannot understand. Whom do you suppose Ken wants to have married? If he hadn't mentioned it right in the very same breath with the blizzard, I wouldn't be so curious."

"Your curiosity is quite natural, Miss Bayley, and it's going to be completely satisfied," the young man said seriously. "I may need your help almost any day now, and so you, too, may share the secret with Dixie and Ken." Then he told the whole story, beginning with the making of the mountain road, two years previous, and ending with his recent flight from the South and his reason for hiding.

[327]

To his surprise, his listener exclaimed: "Mr. Edrington, you are indeed to be congratulated upon your narrow escape. If you know Marlita Arden as well as I do, you are then aware that what she needs most is variety and admiration. I doubt if she would be the comrade sort of wife that I believe you would want." Then, more seriously, "I do not dislike Marlita, understand, but I would be sorry to have my brother Tim marry her."

The girl knew, by the listener's expression that she was amazing him. Nor was she wrong. Marlita Arden was a snob. She would not speak civilly to a woman who earned her own living, and yet this young school-teacher spoke as though she knew the Southern heiress well.

He could not ask how well, and no further information was volunteered. Miss Bayley had risen and was donning her cloak. "I must be going," she said, smiling at him, "for the dusk comes early these winter days."

The young man implored, "Miss Bayley, won't you come often? Have pity on a poor old fossil who's a shut-in."

"Perhaps! Good-by." The teacher looked radiantly young and beautiful as she paused in the open door and smiled back at him.

"She's a princess of a girl," he thought; then he recalled his decision to never fall in love, and he tried to harden his heart.

[328]

CHAPTER FORTY-ONE
A RESOLUTION BROKEN

A never-to-be-forgotten winter followed that first blizzard. Never to be forgotten, at least, by the girl-teacher of the Woodford's Cañon log-cabin school, by the young civil engineer, or by Dixie and Ken Martin. The other children were almost too young to know how portentous those months were.

After the storm there was a spell of clear, cold weather, when the snow-covered valley and mountains sparkled in the pale sunshine, inviting frolic.

For a time Mr. Edrington remained in the cabin, climbing hastily to the loft if sleigh-bells were heard without, but, as the days passed and the wrathful aunt, from whom he was hiding that he need not marry the girl of her choice, did not appear, he became more daring and ventured forth in the full light of day.

[329]

He it was who made, with Ken's help, a wonderful slide down a steep trail which ended at the frozen stream in the valley. Then a marvelous toboggan was constructed, one long and strong enough to take them all on a wild ride from the highway to the valley-bottom.

The young engineer sat in front to steer, and Jimmy-Boy sat just behind and clung to him, and then came, Dixie and Carol, Ken and Miss Bayley.

Once, just for mischief, Mr. Edrington steered into a drift, and they were all half-buried, but they took the ducking good-naturedly.

The young engineer also spent long hours reading in the cabin of his good friend, Josephine Bayley. One of the Martin children accompanied him on these occasions, usually Dixie, who was old enough to enjoy the books that her two older friends liked to read aloud to each other.

[330]

While school was in session the young engineer was not idle, for he had with him his instruments, and many a chart he made as he studied the way to bridge chasms or to tunnel mountains.

February the first was Dixie's birthday. Knowing that her sister and brother could not give her presents, that thoughtful little mother did not remind them of the coming event, and, childlike, they had quite forgotten, for all winter days seemed alike to them. But there was one who had not forgotten, and that one was Miss Bayley. She took Frederick Edrington into her confidence, and a surprise-party was planned and carried out.

The girl-teacher's present to her favorite pupil was in a box, the shape of which aroused much curiosity, but when Dixie saw the gift it contained, her plain face was transfigured.

"Why, that girl is beautiful!" the young engineer said softly to the teacher who stood at his side, watching while the slender maid lifted a bow and violin.

[331]

"Miss Bayley!" How starlike were the eyes that turned toward the beloved friend and benefactress. "Do you really think that some day I shall be able to play?"

There was conviction in the tone of the young woman as she said, "I know it! Some day we shall all listen in rapture, I'll prophesy, and then we'll say proudly, one to another, 'That is *our* Dixie.'"

Going to the girl, Miss Bayley kissed her. "May I take your violin, dear? I studied several musical instruments in school, but cannot play any of them well."

Taking the violin and adjusting it, she played a sweet, simple melody, then explained to the girl, who listened with rapt eagerness, a few of the things that a beginner should know. "Suppose you try to play." The young teacher smiled at the maid, little dreaming that she would comply, but Dixie did not hesitate. She lifted the violin, and, after listening to the strings for a moment, she began to play the same melody that Miss Bayley had but finished. It was imperfectly done, but the young teacher knew that she had been right in believing that the girl was rarely talented.

[332]

"I will teach you all that I know, which isn't much," Miss Bayley said. "Then, when the snow is gone and spring has come, you shall have lessons from some one who is a real musician."

Dixie's cup of happiness seemed full those wintry days, for Carol grew in gentleness and unselfishness, and was ever more loved and more lovable.

"How pleased our father would be!" Dixie said that night as she and Ken were alone in the kitchen after the party. Mr. Edrington had gone with Miss Bayley, to escort her home up the cañon trail, and the younger children were asleep. "Pleased, because we have two such wonderful friends. Three," the girl added brightly, "for surely Mr. Clayburn has been a true friend."

"We have managed to get along quite nicely without our aunt," the boy said as he wound the old grandfather's clock. "I'm just as well pleased that she never did look us up. I'm almost sure we shouldn't like her."

"I don't believe she knows that we even exist," Dixie declared. "Since she never opened any of the letters that were sent to her, how could she know?"

"That's right," Ken agreed. "I wonder what set me to thinking about her? Well, I won't waste any more thought on her. Good-night, Dix."

The girl had started to ascend the ladder to the loft where she slept, but she turned back and kissed the lad as she said: "Ken, you've been a wonderful brother. On birthdays one thinks of those things. Good-night."

The moon arose above old Piney Peak as Miss Bayley and Mr. Edrington left the sheltered cañon trail and turned into the highway.

"I'm going to put out the light in the lantern," the young man said. "We don't need it now, do we?" he smilingly asked after having blown out the flickering flame.

"Where has it gone," she asked, "the light that was there but a moment ago?"

The young man shook his head. "I can't tell you," he declared; "and, Josephine, please don't ask me to think about abstract things just now. I want to tell you something."

The young engineer spoke seriously, almost pleadingly. He did not seem to idealize that he had called his companion by her first name, but Miss Bayley knew it, and she was glad to have him. What had he to tell her? How she hoped—but—even to herself, she would not admit that desire.

For a few moments they walked on in silence. The road was slippery. He held her arm, but still said nothing. At last Miss Bayley peered into his face, trying to get him to lift his eyes from the ground. "I'll not say 'A penny for your thoughts,' that is too trite," she began, "but I do feel sort of left out and lonely. I'm just sure you are trying to figure out how to tunnel through Old Piney and make your walk home with me a quarter of a mile shorter."

He looked up then, his fine eyes laughing, but in them there was an expression which assured the girl that he had not been thinking of tunnels, but of her. Taking her warmly-gloved hand, he said, "Lady of the Sunrise Peak, I'm going away."

She stopped, and her eyes told her surprised disappointment.

"Oh, Mr. Edrington, why? May I ask? I thought you were going to stay here until spring or until you had heard that Marlita Arden had married." She paused questioningly.

"I did intend to, but I'm running away from—something else—myself," he hastened to add. "You see, Miss Bayley, I once made a resolution, and if I stay here I'm afraid I'll break it."

"Indeed? May I know what the resolution was?" They had reached the small cabin beyond the inn, and the girl-teacher paused on the doorstep waiting. What could he say? The liquid-brown eyes that were so expressive were searching his. She knew his answer before it was given.

"I have fallen in love, and I vowed I never would," he said quietly.

"And is that why you are going away?" she inquired.

"No—o," he confessed. "It isn't. I'm going away for one month, Josephine. Not because I want to test my love for you,—I'm sure of that,—but I want you to have time to think—and to be sure." Then he added, "Am I presuming too much when I infer that perhaps you would want to consider caring for me?"

The girl-teacher answered frankly. "Until to-night I have thought of you merely as a comrade, a pal whom I enjoy more than I ever did any one else. But perhaps you are right. If you go away, we can tell better whether it is merely propinquity or love. Good-night."

Frederick Edrington walked slowly back to the cabin, which was dark except for a dim light burning in the room that he now shared with Ken.

He would go to Colorado and inspect some work that was going on there, he decided. He had promised to send in a report of it before spring, and this would afford him that opportunity.

The little Martins were surprised and sorry to hear that their guest was leaving them. "I'll be back in the spring," he told them.

"That's only a month away," Dixie replied at the hour of parting.

CHAPTER FORTY-TWO
AN EVENTFUL SPRING

Spring came, and every mountain cañon held a rushing torrent. The sky was gloriously blue after the long months that it had been leaden-gray, and flowers began to appear in the crevices soon after the snow was gone.

Joy in the heart of the young school-teacher sang with the returning birds. Even the small Martin children seemed to be eagerly expectant.

"I feel as though something ever so nice is going to happen, Miss Bayley, don't you?" Dixie looked up glowingly from the slate on which she was trying to solve a difficult sum.

Her beloved friend and teacher stood at her side. These two had remained after school, that the older Martin girl might catch up with Ken in mathematics.

[338]

"I'd heaps rather write rhymes or sing songs or play on my violin," Dixie confided when at last the slate had been washed clean and replaced in the desk.

"I'm glad," Miss Bayley said as she pinned on her hat, preparing to depart. "You will derive much more joy from the poetry and the music, but arithmetic, too, must be mastered, if you are to go to college."

The girl looked brightly up at her teacher. "I'd have to be living in a fairy-tale to have that happen," she declared. Then laughingly she confessed, "There are only six pennies in the sock under my mattress, and you can't think how hard I have tried to save all winter. However, I might call them a nest-egg toward the future education of the four Martins."

The gold-brown eyes of the girl glowed from beneath the wide brim of her rather shabby hat, but the young teacher saw not the hat but only the radiant young face.

"Dixie," she exclaimed suddenly, "this is the hour that the stage arrives. Let's walk down the cañon road a little way and see if it is coming. Shall we?"

[339]

"I'd love to!" was the glad reply. "And maybe we'll find some wild flowers." Then, when they had started swinging along together, the younger girl asked, looking up at her taller companion, "Miss Bayley, are you expecting some one in particular to come to-day?"

The rosy flush in the teacher's face puzzled Dixie. She had not thought that a romance might exist between Ken's old friend and the young woman whom she so loved.

"No, dear, no one in particular," was the quiet reply, and it was true, for although Miss Bayley had received a letter stating that Frederick Edrington would soon be through with his work of inspection, he had not said when he would revisit the cañon.

They had reached a high point, and Dixie had clambered up on a peak of rocks, that she might have a wider vision. Shading her eyes from the glare of the sun, she looked down into the valley.

[340]

"Surely there is something coming," she called gleefully to the waiting teacher. "I can see it moving among the pine trees." Then, clapping her hands, she added joyfully: "It *is* the stage!

It's out in the clearing, and now it's beginning to climb. I do believe it will pass here in half an hour or so."

Miss Bayley pressed her hand on her heart to try to still its rapid beating. "I can't understand it at all," she thought, "but I seem to feel sure that some one *is* coming on the stage, some one whom I shall be glad to see." Never before had a half hour seemed so long to the two who spent the time searching for flowers among the rocks. Only a few, blue as the sky, had been found, when Dixie stood suddenly alert, listening. "Hear that rumble?" she sang out. "It's the stage just around Old Indian Rock." She pointed to an outjutting boulder below them at the turn in the cañon road. Breathlessly they waited. There were four passengers in the coach, and one was an elderly woman, who, handsomely dressed, sat very erect, and the expression on her proud, aristocratic face assured the two by the roadside that, whoever she might be, the errand that had brought her to the mountains was most displeasing to her.

[341]

The elderly stage-driver waved the hand that held the whip, and beamed down good-naturedly. The young teacher and Dixie smiled and nodded, but although the occupants of the coach must have seen them, they were not at all interested.

The girl heard Miss Bayley sigh. "Dear teacher," she said softly, "won't you come on down to our cabin for supper? There is to be cottage cheese that you like so much, with nice yellow cream on it."

Dixie was convinced that her companion had been expecting some one who had not come.

Josephine Bayley laughed merrily. "You dear little tempter," she said, "of course I'll go." And so hand in hand they descended the trail that led under the great old pines and down to the picturesque log cabin.

Although it was but five o'clock, the little mother at once began to prepare the evening meal. Ken and Jimmy-Boy were out milking the goat, and Carol was over at the Valley Ranch.

"May I set the table?" the teacher inquired.

[342]

Dixie nodded. "Let's use the kept-for-company dishes to-night," she suggested.

"But you promised long ago that you wouldn't call me company," Miss Bayley protested.

"I know I did," Dixie smiled over the big yellow bowl which held the foamy cheese, and into which she was pouring rich cream. "I don't understand the least bit why, but somehow I feel as if to-day were an extra occasion, sort of a party."

"Perhaps because it's the first real spring day that we've had," Miss Bayley announced, as she opened the old walnut sideboard and brought forth the best china. "Your mother liked beautiful things, didn't she, Dixie? This pattern is lovely."

[343]

The girl looked up brightly. "I like it," she replied; then added simply, "I suppose it was hard for Mother to live in a cabin, for all her life had been spent in an old colonial mansion in the South. Our great-aunt, Mrs. James Haddington-Allen, lives there, or, at least, I guess she does. She's never answered any of our letters, but she always writes something on the envelopes before she returns them, so of course she does receive them."

"Have you written to her lately?" Miss Bayley was setting the table as she asked the question. She was surprised at the decided tone in which the small girl replied: "No, I haven't. I never wrote her but once, and that was after we children were left all alone. Our mother had often written, but her letters were always returned unopened."

"Mrs. James Haddington-Allen must be a hard-hearted old dragoness," the girl-teacher thought; but aloud she commented, "If your great-aunt could but see you four children, I am sure she would love you all."

[344]

"She might love Carol because she is beautiful, like our mother, and she'd like Jimmy-Boy too, but Ken and I are regular Martins, so probably our great-aunt wouldn't like us much." To the surprise of the listener, there was a sob in the girl's voice as she continued, "I'd heaps rather our great-aunt would never come, for probably she'd want to take Carol and Jimmy-Boy to her fine Southern home, but she wouldn't want Ken or me. I—I just couldn't live without Carol and Jimmy-Boy. I couldn't. I couldn't!"

Miss Bayley went toward the girl and took her in her arms. "My dear child," she said tenderly, "before I'd let that happen, I would open up my old home in New York on the Hudson and adopt all four of you."

Dixie smiled through her tears. "Goodness!" she said, springing away and wiping her eyes on the towel by the kitchen pump, "the cheese is salty enough as 'tis. I mustn't spill any tears in it."

Dixie had not grasped the meaning of the words she had heard. To her, Miss Bayley was just a poor young woman who had to teach school for a living, and a home in New York on the Hudson presented no picture to the girl who had always lived in the mountains, and who had never been farther away than Genoa. But to Miss Bayley those words had meant much. Why had she never thought of it before, she wondered. If Frederick Edrington never came back to her, if he had found, while away from her, that he had been mistaken, that he did not really care, still her life need not be empty.

[345]

She would go back to New York and take these four children with her. The great old salon that had been in darkness since the death of her parents would ring once again with laughter and song. Then when her brother Tim came back from his three years at sea, there would be a happy home waiting for him. The picture delighted the girl-teacher, and she began to sing as she placed the supper dishes on the best table-cloth.

Carol came in, bringing a bunch of early flowers from a sunny, sheltered garden on the Valley Ranch.

"Oh, how pretty!" Miss Bayley exclaimed. "They are just what we need for the middle of the table."

The younger girl looked mystified. "Is there going to be a party? Is somebody extra coming?"

"No, dear, just we five," Miss Bayley began, but the small girl interrupted with, "But, teacher, you've put out six plates and everything."

"So I have!" The girl-teacher actually blushed. But before she could explain, even to herself, why she had done this, Dixie called excitedly, "Carol, skip to the door and see who's coming. Ken's waving his cap and shouting to some one coming down the cañon trail."

CHAPTER FORTY-THREE
THE UNEXPECTED GUEST

Dixie, a mixing-spoon in her hand, and Carol, still holding the flowers, darted to the open door and peered up the trail that led toward the highway.

Ken had placed the pail of milk on the ground and was racing toward the newcomer, shouting his joy. Jimmy, not to be outdone, was hopping up and down, uttering shrill cries of glee, though he had not the least idea who might be coming.

Miss Bayley stood by the table, her hand pressed to her heart. All day there had been within her a prophetic feeling of some joy in store for her. She listened breathlessly until she heard the name that Dixie announced. "It's Mr. Edrington, as sure as anything!" she called in delight. Although the young engineer was Ken's particular friend, the other three Martins loved him dearly.

The young man threw his knapsack to the ground and held out both arms to receive all four of them. Even Dixie, unconscious of the mixing-spoon that she held, ran down the trail to meet him. The young teacher alone stayed within the cabin.

"Oh-ee, Uncle Ed, but we're glad you've come home," Carol said. That was the name the young man had suggested that they call him.

"Home," he thought. "What a wonderful word that is!" He had never really had a home, for, although his aunt had seemed to care for him, she had been too nervous to have children around, and so he had been sent to a military academy, and from then, until he became a full-fledged engineer, nine months of every year he had been in a school of some sort, and even the three months of vacation had been spent in hotels at fashionable resorts. This log cabin in the Nevada mountains had been more of a home than he had ever before known.

"Where's Miss Bayley?" Carol asked, looking back at the open door in surprise. "Why didn't she come out?"

The girl-teacher heard. She couldn't have explained to herself why she had remained in hiding when she so longed to greet her good friend.

"Here I am," she called gayly, appearing at that moment on the porch. With a glad exclamation the young engineer leaped forward, both hands outstretched. "Josephine," he said in a low voice, "have you decided? Did you miss me?"

Miss Bayley had become mistress of her emotions. "Of course we all missed you," she said, looking frankly into the fine, gray eyes that told her so much. Then she added, turning to the older Martin girl, "Dear, hadn't we better have supper now?" Then, to the younger, "You see, Carol, I did well to set out a sixth plate."

[350]

The young man smiled as he followed the young woman indoors, and began to wash at the kitchen pump, as he had been wont to do in the days when he was one of the family, for, try as she might to appear indifferent, Josephine Bayley's manner and expression had assured him that his love was returned.

Such a merry supper followed. Mr. Edrington had many an adventure to relate. He had met interesting and queer characters in the Rockies, where he had been inspecting the putting-through of a tunnel.

The meal was half over when Dixie suddenly thought of something. "Mr. Edrington," she exclaimed, "there was a very fine-looking old lady on the stage-coach to-night. I forgot to mention, it. Your coming sort of drove all my other thoughts away. Do you think that maybe it might be your aunt?"

To the surprise of the two older Martin children, the young man beamed happily upon them. "I hope it is!" he declared. Then, reaching out his strong brown hand, he placed it on the slender white one that was lying on the table near him. "If it is my aunt, then without delay I shall be able to introduce to her my future wife, Josephine Bayley."

[351]

Children take wonderful things quite as a matter of course. Why not, since they can believe in fairies?

"Oh! Oh! I am so glad! Then we can call our dear teacher Aunt Josephine, can't we?" eagerly asked glowing-eyed Dixie.

That night as the young couple walked up the cañon road together, Frederick Edrington for the first time told of the fortune that his father had left him.

"I am glad that I have it, for your sake," he said to the girl at his side, "for it will enable me to give you many luxuries. Whatever things you have desired through the years, now you shall have."

"Thank you Frederick," the girl replied, realizing fully for the first time that her fiancé believed her to be a poor young person who had to work for a living. As they passed the inn, they could look into the brightly-lighted parlor. There they saw several people, but only one was near enough to the window to be recognized.

"It is my aunt," the young man said, "and I suspect that Marlita Arden is with her."

At the doorstep of the cabin they paused. The young man held out his hand. "Josephine," he said, "will you go with me in the morning to the inn, that I may introduce to my aunt and her friends the sweetest little woman in the world, who is soon to be my wife?"

The girl-teacher could not have told why she replied, "But, Frederick, your aunt will be so disappointed because you are to marry some one who does not belong to her world, some one who is obscure and—"

Earnestly the young man interrupted: "It is for me to say what manner of maid I shall marry; but, dear, if you would rather not go,—if it will place you in an unpleasant position,—I will not ask you to accompany me. I will go alone."

The girl looked up at him radiantly, and there was an amused expression in her lovely eyes that he could not understand.

"I shall be glad to go, Frederick," she said. "I'll be ready early. Good-night."

CHAPTER FORTY-FOUR
CLEARING UP MYSTERIES

While Josephine Bayley prepared her breakfast the next morning, every now and then she paused to laugh gleefully. Was she doing wrong to deceive the fine man who loved her so dearly? And yet, after all, she had not deceived him. He had never once asked her who her father had been. He had merely jumped to the conclusion that she was poor because she was teaching school in Woodford's Cañon. After all, that was a natural inference.

He had completely forgotten, or so it seemed, that on the first day of their acquaintance Josephine had mentioned that she had known Marlita Arden. The truth was that Frederick had not forgotten. He had, however, satisfied his own curiosity as to the manner in which the two girls had met. Marlita had a younger sister, Gladys Louise, and, as he thought of her, he recalled that she had a governess named Josephine. He had never seen her, but since his Josephine knew Marlita intimately, she probably had lived in their home as governess to the younger Arden girl.

As the young engineer walked toward the cabin beyond the inn at nine that morning, with each stride his decision grew stronger. His aunt, he knew, would scorn any girl who earned her own living, but she would be especially rude, he was convinced, to a young woman who had been governess in the home of one of her friends.

After all, perhaps it would be kinder not to take Josephine Bayley with him when he went to see his aunt at the inn. He could announce his intention to marry whom he would, and let the matter rest there, but, to his surprise, when he told the girl he loved that he wished to spare her possible humiliation, she looked so truly disappointed that he exclaimed: "Why, Josephine, you don't *want* to go, do you? I thought you were merely accompanying me because I had requested it."

[355]

She smiled at him, and in her expression there was no trace of timidity. "I'm not the least bit afraid of dragoness aunts," she assured him. Then she added, "If you'll be seated a moment, I'll don my best spring hat and coat."

Five minutes later the girl emerged from her porch room, and the young man leaped to his feet, gazing as though at a vision.

"How beautiful you are in that silvery gray," he said.

The small hat was wreathed with crushed roses, and the cloak, of soft clinging material, was cut in the latest fashion.

At another time the young man might have been puzzled, but his mind was too full of one thing just then to admit of questionings.

"I'm glad you look so nicely," he confided as they started out, "for even though mine aunt will, of course, spurn me for not wedding the girl of her choice, in her heart of hearts she will have to agree that I have chosen the more beautiful one for my bride."

[356]

The color in Josephine's cheeks deepened, although it may have been a reflection of the rose-tulle lining of her hat.

In the meantime the strangers at the inn had inquired if Frederick Edrington were staying there.

Although Mr. Enterprise Twiggly well knew the young man whom Ken called Uncle Ed, he did not associate the two names, and replied that he knew "no such person."

Mrs. Edrington and her companions were in the parlor of the inn, awaiting the coming of the stage, when the two young people arrived. Josephine requested that she be permitted to remain in the outer office while Frederick went alone to meet his aunt.

The four occupants of the plainly furnished room turned as the door opened, and the young engineer was somewhat surprised to see that one of them was no other than Lord Dunsbury. The two girls were Marlita Arden and her younger sister, Gladys Louise. Frederick regretted this, since his Josephine undoubtedly had been her governess. Perhaps the girl he loved ought to be told to slip back to her cabin home, that she might escape whatever humiliation would be in store for her, were she to meet the snobbish Ardens.

[357]

"I'm so glad to see you again," said Marlita.

"More than pleased I assure you," rather coldly added the young Englishman.

Frederick crossed the room to where his aunt was standing, and spoke with her for several moments. The others, watching, could see the angry flush mounting to the face of the older woman. Then, unable to listen longer in silence, she turned toward the curious group and exclaimed: "My nephew informs me that he is engaged to marry some girl he has met here in the mountains. A woodcutter's daughter, I suppose. Being well acquainted with his stubbornness, I know that he will do as he wishes in the matter."

[358]

Marlita shrugged her silk-clad shoulders as she said, "Do you know, Aunt Delia, I really would like to see the mountain maid who has won the heart of friend Frederick." Then, turning to the young man, she added with a tantalizing smile, "However, I doubt if he would care to exhibit his rural fiancée." This remark had the effect desired.

"You are wrong Marlita," Frederick declared vehemently. "I should be proud to present my future wife to the queen of England, were that possible. If you will be seated, I will soon return with the young woman about whom we are speaking."

It was a tense moment for the two who were most interested. The aunt moved to the window and looked out. Marlita leaned against the mantle, tapping her fingers nervously thereon.

It was not very complimentary to her that Frederick Edrington should prefer a mountaineer's daughter to the heiress of Colonel Arden's millions.

They all glanced toward the closed door when they heard Frederick returning. Gladys Louise was the only one pleased with the little drama that was being enacted. How she did hope that Fred's fiancée would prove to be the picturesque type of mountain maid that she had read about in romantic stories! Perhaps, though, they were only to be found in Switzerland.

[359]

However, there was no further time for speculating. The door was opening, and in another moment they would know.

Josephine Bayley had never looked lovelier than she did when she entered the parlor of the inn, her head held high. Although her lips were not smiling, surely an amused expression was lurking in the depths of her clear hazel eyes.

Before Frederick Edrington could introduce his fiancée to his aunt, Gladys Louise, with a glad cry of recognition, leaped forward, both hands outstretched. "Oh, you dear, darling

Josephine!" she exclaimed. "Why didn't you tell us where you disappeared to when you left so suddenly?"

And so the young engineer's surmise had been correct. His fiancée had been this impulsive girl's governess. What would his aunt say? He glanced at Marlita, to see how she would welcome one who had lived in her home in a paid capacity. The proud girl's expression was hard to understand.

[360]

Then, to his surprise, Josephine made the first advance. Crossing the room, she held out her hand as she said: "Marlita, dear, please try to be glad for my happiness. You and I were room-mates at boarding-school, and now—"

She said no more, for the girl to whom she had spoken drew herself away coldly. "You are not honest, Josephine Bayley," she said, "posing as a woodcutter's daughter when—"

The young teacher shook her head. "I have not posed," she replied quietly. "Frederick has asked no questions concerning my family." Then, again holding out her hand, she pleaded, "Marlita, won't you be my friend?"

But the girl whom she addressed tossed her head and left the room, beckoning her sister and Lord Dunsbury to follow, which they did.

When the three were alone, Frederick, whose astonishment had seemed to render him speechless, apologized. "Pardon me, Aunt Delia," he said, "permit me to introduce to you my fiancée."

[361]

"We'll waive the formality of an introduction," replied the woman, who, through half-closed eyes, had been watching the little drama.

Then, turning to the girl in gray, she asked, "Are you the daughter of William Wallace Bayley whose summer home is in the Orange Hills, and whose winter home is in New York on the Hudson?"

"I am," was the quiet reply.

It was Frederick Edrington's turn to be amazed, but his aunt was continuing: "I thought so. With my former husband, Mr. James Haddington-Allen, I frequently visited your home when you were a very small child."

The young school-teacher stepped forward, as she asked eagerly: "You—are you Mrs. James Haddington-Allen? Frederick has always spoken of you as Mrs. Edrington."

"Naturally, since that is my present name. Mr. Allen died long ago, and two years later I married Frederick's uncle. But pray, Miss Bayley, why has the discovery of my former name occasioned you so much concern?"

[362]

"Because you are also the aunt of the four children named Martin who are our protégés here in the mountains," Frederick began. But the face of the older woman hardened. "You are mistaken," she said. "The children of whom you speak are related to my first husband, but in no way to me; and, since he is dead, I see no reason why I should look up his poor relatives, and, what is more, I shall not do so."

The young man's voice was almost severe when he asked, "You knew of their need, then?"

"Some banker wrote me last year concerning these children, and I replied that I was not at all interested in hearing about them. However, I thought the name of their town was Genoa." Then, turning to the school-teacher, who was finding it very hard to listen quietly, the older woman said, "Miss Bayley, if you will give up this ridiculous notion of teaching school and will come with me, I will forgive you both and take you into my home, but mind, I wish never again to hear the name of Martin."

[363]

"I thank you for your offer, but I have made other plans," was Josephine's reply. "When the spring term is finished, I shall return to my New York home and take with me the four Martin children."

"Then, as there is nothing more to be said, I will bid you good-morning." Haughtily saying this, the aunt left the room, and did not even glance at her second husband's nephew.

"Shall we tell the children?" was Josephine's first question as they left the inn.

"No," Frederick replied. "Mrs. Edrington is their aunt only by marriage, as she is mine." Then he added, "Dearest, what a wonderful home you and I are to have with such nice kiddies in it."

"Aren't we?" the girl smiled up at him. "We shall be happy just because we are all together." Then she continued, "I want to make those four little Martins the happiest children in all the world."

THE END

BOOKS
BY
GRACE MAY NORTH

ADELE DORING BOOKS
Cloth. 12mo. Jackets and Illustrations in Colors.

ADELE DORING OF THE SUNNYSIDE CLUB
ADELE DORING ON A RANCH

ADELE DORING AT BOARDING-SCHOOL
ADELE DORING IN CAMP
ADELE DORING AT VINEYARD VALLEY

DIXIE MARTIN

Jacket in colors and Illustrated.

LOTHROP, LEE & SHEPARD CO., BOSTON

Transcriber's Notes

- Copyright notice provided as in the original printed text—this e-text is public domain in the country of publication.
- Silently corrected palpable typos; left non-standard spellings and dialect unchanged.
- Moved promotional material to the end of the text.
- In the text versions, included italics inside _underscores_ (the HTML version replicates the format of the original.)

Made in the USA
Las Vegas, NV
18 November 2021